CHAIN REACTION

A TECHNOTHRILLER

GERALD M. KILBY

OUTER PLANET
MEDIA

D1409991

For notifications on upcoming books, and access to my FREE starter library,
please join my Readers Group at www.geraldmkilby.com.

CONTENTS

AUTHOR RETROSPECTIVE

I recently read a book by Arthur C. Clarke, *The City and the Stars*, and discovered that it was an extensive revision of his first novel, *Against the Fall of Night*. Apparently, he revisited the book several years after becoming an accomplished sci-fi author and realized that he had improved considerably as a writer in the intervening period. And so he set about rewriting his first novel with the benefit of his deeper knowledge and experience.

This got me thinking, and I soon found myself revisiting my very first novel, *Fusion* (later *Reaction*). I've always liked the plot and the characters in this book but I was never quite happy with the flow of the story. There seemed to be too much going on and not all of it had an obvious connection. Even before I published it, I had given a printout to friends to read for feedback and it was only after, that I realized I had accidentally left out one complete chapter. I had provided them with an incomplete book — no one noticed. This should have told me something, but I simply didn't have the knowledge or experience back then to understand the significance of this. Nevertheless, I did have an instinctive feeling that the novel was a bit clunky and made an early attempt to resolve it by separating out the secondary character story as a short-story (*Extraction*). In reality though, while I knew something was not right with the story structure, I did not quite know how to fix it.

Yet, taking inspiration from Clarke, I went back to my first novel again after several years and over a dozen novels later, I could instantly see where it went wrong, but more importantly, this time I knew how to make it a much better book. So I rolled up my sleeves and embarked on a complete root and branch rewrite of my very first novel.

I have always enjoyed the characters in the novel, they have a special place in my heart, and so I took great pleasure in revisiting their story and giving them the book they truly deserve. Some scenes have been removed and some new additions have been written. What's more, every sentence in the novel has been gone over with a fine-toothed comb and honed to the best of my ability. In the end, while it's still essentially the same story, it has in my mind, a much better flow and is now the technothriller I had wanted to write all those years ago but couldn't quite get there.

I also took the opportunity to update the technology depicted in the book. A lot has happened with ITER and fusion in general since the book was first published. Breakthroughs in fusion experiments have been announced at a rapid clip recently, inching us ever closer to the holy grail of a sustainable, energy positive, fusion reactor.

ITER is still under construction, no surprise there. But it has passed some crucial milestones and has now entered the assembly phase, which is expected to take another few years. The good news is that the main components have been fabricated and now it's all down to making sure they fit together as intended. Expected date for completion is 2025 but I imagine this will get pushed out. Nevertheless, it's very much on the home straight, and barring any "catastrophe," it should be generating first plasma in the latter half of this decade.

In the novel, I have a Chinese consortium developing a competing fusion reactor technology, but in reality, ITER is truly international with the following countries deeply involved in the development of the project: European Union, US, China, India, Japan, South Korea, and Russia. All of whom share in the cost of construction.

That said, a fusion reactor based on helium-3 is not only theoretically possible (in so far as any fusion reactor is theoretically possible) but it also has the potential to be far more efficient with virtually no waste and no radiation. However, most if not all the current crop of experimental reactors use some combination of the hydrogen isotopes of tritium and deuterium, including ITER. Deuterium is abundant in sea water and tritium can be created during the reaction. Helium-3, on the other hand, is almost nonexistent on Earth. Hence any discussion of H3 reactors soon moves onto mining it on the Moon, where it's abundant in the top-layer regolith.

If you've ever watched the movie *Moon*, staring the awesome Sam Rockwell and directed by Duncan Jones, the plot is based on mining helium-3.

"In the near future, Lunar Industries has made a fortune after an oil crisis by building Sarang Station, a facility on the far side of the Moon to mine the alternative fuel helium-3 from lunar soil."

Ever wondered why there's a race to get back to the moon?

MareNostrum, the supercomputer in Barcelona, has also had a major upgrade. At the time of my first research and writing, it was on its third iteration (MareNostrum 3) and had a peak performance of 1.1 petaflops.

It's now moving toward its fifth iteration (MareNostrum 5) capable of a whopping 205 petaflops, making it one of the most powerful in the world. Currently the US-based Summit, located at the Oak Ridge National Laboratory, is top of the table with 143.5 petaflops. However, by the time the new MareNostrum 5 goes live, it may be pipped to number one. But I don't think it will ever fall from the top slot as the world's most beautiful. And yes, it is actually built inside an old 19th century church. Google it ;-)

Insect drones, of the type I describe in the book, are still very experimental. Also known as Micro Air Vehicles (MAV). The concept of tiny spy drones has prompted research and development efforts by various state agencies. But most of what exists at the moment are just early prototypes.

The best visualization that I've seen so far of winged vehicle (ornithopter) is in the recent *DUNE* movie. I had always been fascinated by this concept ever since reading the book, many years ago, and for me one of the best parts of the movie was the rendering of the "thropters" in flight. In my own book, the vision I had of the insect drones was very much based on the dragonfly image, similar to the thropters in DUNE, albeit on a miniature scale. They just seemed so elegant to me. Not surprising since they have over 300 million years of evolutionary design built in.

I also wanted to make the insect drones deadly, and the idea of using poison darts came to me while watching a documentary on the development of modern medical anaesthetics. Back in the early days, not too long ago, if you needed surgery then the best pain management you could get was a bottle of whiskey and a stick to bite down on.

It was only through the early study of curare, a botanical concoction used by the people of Central and South America to paralyze their prey when hunting, that modern anaesthesia began to take shape. It was these concoctions that were used in early surgical experiments, along with other drugs such as cocaine, ether, and chloroform.

In smaller doses, curare will paralyze the muscles, in larger doses, it will also paralyze the diaphragm and the patient/victim will die from asphyxiation. However, if the patient can be kept breathing manually, then curare could prove to be very useful in surgical operations. In an early experiment to test this theory back in 1825, Charles Waterton, an English naturalist, kept a donkey named Wouralia alive by artificial respiration with bellows. Fortunately, Wouralia survived and went on to live a full and contented life.

So what about fusion energy? Sadly, the reality is that it still remains a vision for the future. Contrary to all the recent headlines and hype, no one has yet managed to get more out of a fusion reaction than they put in. The best so far is the Joint European Torus (JET) in the UK that produced 59 megajoules of energy back in February 2022. To put this in perspective, this is only enough to boil around 60 kettles of water, and it required over three times the energy to produce it, so we still have a long way to go.

That said, ITER still remains our best bet to achieve the goal of sustainable, energy positive fusion reaction. Once completed it should produce 10 times more energy out than is input. The primary reason for this is its vast size. Yet, it's still only an experimental reactor and is not designed to produce electricity. Its purpose is as a pathfinder, showing the way for future fusion energy generators to be built. In short, we're not there yet. But I've no doubt that we will get there, probably sooner than we think.

I do hope you enjoy this new revised edition of my very first technothriller. And who knows, if the feedback is positive, I may even write a follow-up adventure.

1

SHIPS THAT PASS

C harles Gardner was three hours steady sailing on this course from making port at Monaco and, with a bit of luck, would be safely inside the harbor before the storm hit. He was sitting in the snug confines of the chart table onboard his 50-ft sailing sloop, his brooding face illuminated by the reflected glare of a laptop screen and various navigation instruments arrayed around him. Scratching his three-day-old stubble, he took another sip of whiskey and contemplated his position.

Outside, a warm damp Sirocco blew in from the east, bringing with it the threat of an early summer storm across the northern Mediterranean Sea. The night air was hot and humid, and heavy clouds hung low, blocking out much of the light from the heavens. Inside, the oppressive weather fueled the lone sailor's general mood of melancholy, a mood he had not afforded himself for some time. But every now and then, dark clouds would gather in his head, and each time he would fight them off. Someday, he knew he would have to face them, he would have to sail his soul through the storm, feel the fear, as it were, if he ever wanted to come out the other side to a better day. But not today, not this night. *Time enough for that*, he thought.

Beep! Beep!

It was nearly three months since he'd left port at Southampton on a solo cruise around the Mediterranean and over three years since his wife Jenny had died. He still felt the loss. He felt it so deeply that he was afraid of it, afraid of where it might take him if he went there. He imagined conversations that his children might have with their friends around a coffee or a glass of wine. *How's he doing after your mom? Oh, he's keeping busy.*

He used to say the very same thing about his father when his own mother died. But in truth, he never understood its full meaning. How could he? He was young then, and youth has better things to do, it has life to live. He didn't understand the loss, the loneliness, and, if he were being really true to himself, the sheer soul-crushing emptiness. Perhaps that's just the way it plays out, to run the full gamut of emotional storm clouds until there are no more left to battle. You either come out the other side into bright sunshine and a better day, or you simply don't come out at all. In the meantime, he kept busy.

BEEP! BEEP!

"Huh?" he tilted his head up from the weather reports on

the laptop and fixed his gaze on a small radar monitor—the source of the beeping alerts. Illuminated on the screen was another vessel, not a sailing boat, too big an image for that, around one nautical mile dead ahead directly in his path—he would have to change course. Fortunately, it was still far enough away not to be an imminent danger, but what unnerved him was that he had not noticed the beeping. *How long has that been going on? It should alert me before being this close, how come I didn't notice?* he thought as he wiped a hand across his forehead. *I need to wake up and get a grip.* He downed the remains of his whiskey and came back to the real world.

Charles scanned the data readout of the distant boat. It didn't look like it was moving, so it was probably not a merchant vessel. More likely it was a luxury yacht, and a pretty big one judging by the size of the image. This was not unusual because the entire northern Mediterranean was dotted with the floating mansions of the fabulously wealthy.

What is it doing just sitting there with a bad storm heading this way? he wondered.

He checked his speed over the ground. He was doing a little under five knots, around five and a half miles an hour, so he had about ten minutes until he sailed right up the transom of the other boat. This gave him plenty of time to check it out.

Beep! Beep!

He silenced the alert and went up on deck. Dead ahead, against a sea of darkness, a smudge of illumination outlined a huge luxury yacht. He fished out a set of low-light binoculars from the helm locker to get a better view.

From the enhanced image, he could make out the bulk of the brooding monster as it slumbered silently in almost complete darkness—motionless and forbidding. He examined it for a minute and was about to put down the binoculars when a crack of light appeared on the rear of the boat as a stern bay door slowly opened. In tandem with it, a broad diving platform started to extend from just above the waterline. Along the top of the stern, he could now make out the name, Helios.

Someone going for an evening swim? he wondered.

A group of figures came through the door and out on to the platform, their shapes silhouetted against the interior lights. Charles could make out three men and one woman. He probably would have looked away at that point, leaving the revelers to their late-night swim, and returned to tending his own boat. But his interest was piqued by the movement of the woman. He couldn't be sure, but it seemed as if she had no arms. Then he suddenly realized that her hands were tied behind her back.

"What the..." He zoomed in a bit more to get a better look.

One of the figures grabbed the woman's hair, pulling her head back as he kicked her in the back of the legs. She collapsed down on her knees, facing the two figures.

Charles braced himself against the cockpit bulkhead, trying to steady the binoculars as best he could. At this magnification, the view bounced around quite a bit with the roll of the boat.

One of the men took something from his pocket and pointed it at the forlorn woman. There was a bright flash and her head exploded as she was flung violently back across the platform.

"Holy shit!" Charles heard no sound, no aural cue to authenticate the scene he had just witnessed—it was like a silent dream. His eye sockets began to hurt from pressing the binoculars hard to his face, so he lowered them and rubbed his eyes. After a second or two, he looked back again.

Two figures were wrapping the woman's body in something. Then they kicked the bundle over the side of the platform and into the sea. A blot of dull white foam radiated from where she entered the water.

Charles lowed the binoculars again as his mind tried to comprehend the implications of what he had just witnessed. His heart was racing, he could feel it thumping in his chest. He shook his head and rubbed his eyes. Then he dared one more look back. The three figures were still there, one was hosing down the platform, one was smoking a cigarette, and one was looking out to sea—directly at Charles's sailboat.

Dammit. Better get the hell out of here, he thought as he grabbed the wheel in a panic and swung to starboard. The mainsail banged over on a new tack, and he flipped the switch to winch over the jib for the new course. The sails flapped loudly, then steadied. He set the sails to pick up speed, and a new energy coursed through hull of the Ave Maria as it headed eastward away from the Helios—away from the horror.

There's no way they could have seen me, is there? he wondered.

2

PORT HERCULE

First came the faintest glimmer of moonlight, shadowed by nocturnal clouds as they moved and separated, their vague shapes like ghosts escaping the celestial brightness. Then, a faint dull white blot of foam on a bubbling sea, and from its center rose the woman. Her face a twisted contorted mask of pain, her hair matted with blood and seaweed, her dress a tattered fragment. Into the gathering light, she rose and grew in form and substance. She looked at him and offered him her hand, arm outstretched. "Save me!" Her cry was shrill and faint in the night. Charles went to raise his hand in concert with hers, but couldn't, as if his veins had filled with lead. Then her face transmuted, and her form morphed through a procession of strange impossible shapes, benign and beguiling, until, finally, a soft glow emanated from her soul as she escaped her watery chrysalis and revealed herself in all her brilliant glory. It was Jenny, his dear departed wife, his soulmate, his love. Her arm outstretched. "Save me. Save me, Charlie."

If only he could move his limbs, just reach her hand, so near, almost within his grasp. Why could he not move?

Her face then beheld betrayed confusion, why would he not reach out and save her? The sea rose in anger all around as the wind broke against her, the tempest building in ferocity. "Save me..." Her voice was lost in the noise of the maelstrom that engulfed her. A terrible noise, a blinding flash, a crack of thunder, and then she was gone.

He awoke.

Charles's body was drenched in sweat, soaking the bed sheets. The clock blinked 4:37 am. He had moored late the previous evening as the storm began to break. The noise was the rain on the roof of the yacht. A thunderous cacophony, as if the heavens had unleashed a downpour of stones. It was deafening. He sat up in bed, the cabin hot and stuffy, and he wiped the sweat from his face. Then a chill ran through his body, and he shook. After a while, he got up and went into the galley to make some tea, the execution of the ritual calming him. He sat at the table and gathered his wits before attempting to go back to sleep, the dream slowly fading in his memory as the storm above abated. After some time, he didn't know how long, he ventured to his bunk and fell back asleep.

The morning sounds of the busy harbor of Port Hercule in Monaco filtered down through Charles's fitful slumber and percolated into his subconscious. His eyes opening slowly as the light of a bright sunny day finally coaxed him awake. Gathering himself together, he headed up top to get some early morning air and clear his head. He needed to think. Standing now on the deck of the *Ave Maria*, mug of tea in hand, he soaked up the sun's heat and surveyed his new surroundings.

He was berthed on the southwestern side of the harbor with the stern of the boat facing onto the walkway of a floating marina. A long line of sailing boats were berthed on either side of him, and beyond those rose a horizon of luxury yachts, some gigantic, some merely enormous, arrayed like a gleaming white citadel. In the distance, the city of Monte Carlo sat at the foot of the hills to the north and east.

The marina walkway was busy with people. Some were cleaning, fixing, delivering, going to and fro, busying themselves servicing the needs of boats and their owners. Others were tourists, looking, pointing, dreaming. The owners and their crew were spending their time chatting, enjoying the sun and trying not to look intimidated by the guy next door with a bigger boat.

Charles stretched his arms and shoulders, scratched his four-day-old stubble, and contemplated what to do, the memory of the previous night still etched in his retina. *Be careful,* he thought. He was sailing in dangerous waters, who knows who those people were on that yacht last night.

After some time, a plan of action formulated in his head, probably not a very good one, but a plan nevertheless. He finished his tea, went below and had a shower and a good scrub up. Feeling somewhat more refreshed, he threw a few essentials into a small rucksack and headed up top. From a refashioned stern locker, he took out his fold-up motorbike, although the term *motorbike* was a little ambitious since it was tiny, with a top speed of 45 km, just big enough to hold his tall fame. He unfolded the bike on the walkway and got on, fired it up, and gave it a few revs to wake it up a bit. The little two-stroke whined into life. He then fished out his phone, set a location into Google Maps, and clipped it on the handlebars. Lastly, he set the alarm on the boat. "See you later, boat," he said to himself as he headed off in the direction of the town of Nice, some 20 km across the French border to the west.

An hour later, Charles Gardner was sitting outside a street café, down along a maintenance harbor on the edge of the port. It was quiet. Charles picked a seat out of earshot of the only other customer and ordered an espresso from a sleek waitress with a studied aloof boredom. He waited until she was gone and cast a quick glance at the only other customer to ensure that he wasn't paying any attention to him. He then reached into his rucksack and took out a new burner phone that he had acquired in a phone shop along the way. He snapped in a new SIM card and powered it on. As the little phone booted up, he was struck by the old Nokia handshake logo, finding it somewhat prophetic in the context of what he was about to do. "A helping hand," he said to himself. He keyed in the number of the Monaco Harbor Police, took another quick look around, and hit the dial button.

3

INSPECTOR MADELAINE DUCHAMP

Detective Inspector Madelaine Duchamp leaned against the open door of her small office balcony on the third floor of the Monaco Harbor Police Building. Gazing over the hustle and bustle of the Monte Carlo morning in the aftermath of last night's storm, she took another deep drag on her cigarette followed by a long slow exhale. *Another day in La-La Land,* she thought.

She had been assigned to this posting by the French Police Department around a year ago as a kind of thank you for services rendered to the state. She had taken a bullet for France in an attack on their embassy in Bamako, Mali. Although not before she shot and killed two of the terrorists. But it was slim solace because her husband had been killed in the attack. She was the only one to come out alive. So, they patched her up, handed her a medal, and gave her an extremely low-stress assignment.

In reality, it was a retirement home for traumatized heroes. That's because nothing ever happened in Monaco. It had the lowest crime rate of any country, and its murder rate was approximately one per decade.

She took another drag of her cigarette and, in her mind, reviewed all her current *high-level* cases. These consisted mostly of minor break-ins, bust-ups, and chasing the Paparazzi out of town. Oh, and then there was Princess Maud and the case of the missing dog, Fluffy-Wuffy. She gave a smile and shook her head. "Christ," she said to herself. "La-La Land."

Her phone rang. Madelaine snapped it of her belt, looked at the screen, and was relived to find that it wasn't Princess Maud wanting another update on the case. Instead, it was Madelaine's assistant, Maria. "Yeah?" she answered.

"I got a John Smith on the line, looking to talk to you about a possible murder. Yeah, you heard that right, murder. I'd say he's probably a nut-job, but he asked for you specifically. Do you want to take it?"

Madelaine sighed. "Okay, put him through."

She moved inside the office, away from the hissing and bubbling of street noise, to concentrate better on the call. Nut-job or not, it would at least be entertaining.

"Inspector Madelaine Duchamp here... I see... Last night... And did you get the name of this yacht?... The Helios." Madelaine's eyes widened. She knew that name.

"I'll need you to come in and give a statement, can you do that, Mr. Smith?"

There was silence at the other end.

"Mr. Smith?" The line went dead.

"Damn!" She went to her desk and stabbed a button on the intercom. "Maria, get me the recording of that call and bring it in here immediately."

A few minutes later, Madelaine leaned over her desk and pressed the stop icon on the recording. "Well, what do you think?"

"Nut-job" said Maria who was currently sitting opposite, tapping a pen on a bunch of papers resting on her knee—she liked paper. Madelaine regarded her as one of those lucky creatures that went through life with a cheery efficiency. She imagined that nothing bad had ever happened to her throughout her young life, and probably nothing bad ever would. In a way, she envied her.

"Seriously though."

"Seriously? Nut-job."

Madelaine sighed and sat back in her chair. "Yeah, it's probably complete nonsense. But just humor me, even if it's only academic."

Maria smiled.

"Have we got anything on the phone number?" Madelaine prompted.

Maria considered her notes. "The call came from a cellphone somewhere in Nice, prepaid, new number."

"So, what does that tell us?"

"Eh…" said Maria.

Madelaine sighed, then stood up, walked over to the balcony, and looked out across the main harbor of Monte Carlo at the luxury yacht, the Helios—its vast bulk dominating most of the other yachts. "And what about our caller, what can we tell about him? Why did he ask for me?"

Maria's brain was working hard, trying to operate in areas it was not familiar with, speculation being one of them.

"Sailor!" she announced. "He said he was sailing. I mean, he was not on a power boat," she offered.

Madelaine looked at Maria and raised an eyebrow. "Very astute, Maria, we'll make a detective out of you yet. So why ask for me?"

"He probably picked it out from the website or a journal— just random."

"I don't believe in random," replied Madelaine.

"If the call is from Nice, then our *Mr. Smith* might be moored there," ventured Maria.

"Which puts him conveniently out of our jurisdiction," said Madelaine. "However, maybe some of the other boats that came in last night saw something. It's worth a shot. Who's doing the customs checks this morning?"

Maria consulted her clipboard. "Jacques and his crew."

"Tell him we'll join them. We'll ask a few questions and see what pops up."

"Okay, will do." She turned to go.

"One other thing, Maria. Find out the last port of call of the Helios and get the passenger manifest."

"Okay, will do too."

She was heading out the door again when she hesitated and turned back to Madelaine. "Eh...are you coming to the art exhibition this evening?"

It took Madelaine a minute to figure out what she was talking about. Then it dawned on her. It was the Annual Royal Art Exhibition, and Maria's boyfriend had been selected to exhibit.

"Oh, eh...no, sorry, I can't make it. Got to pick up my son, Leon, after school. He's got a hockey match, said I'd come along and give some moral support."

"No problem, maybe some other time then?"

"Sure, maybe."

Maria's phone pinged. She glanced at the screen, then raised her eyebrows to Madelaine as she answered. "Sorry, Princess Maud, she's terribly busy right now. Yes, yes, we're doing everything we can to find Fluffy-Wuffy. We currently have a team of agents searching the entire Principality. Yes, I'm sure she'll be fine."

La-La Land, thought Madelaine.

4

OF MICE AND MEN

A new and long-awaited day was beginning on the Moon over Tycho Crater as an alien dawn broke over the jagged rim of the massive lunar crater. It advanced slowly down the fractured interior slope and onward across the great expanse of the desolate and lifeless central plateau.

Waiting in the shadows of the now receding celestial night sat several small solar-powered machines, dormant and unmoving, robotic reptilians waiting for the light to arrive to energize them into industry. As one by one the sun's rays bathed their solar panels with energy-giving photons, dormant circuits buzzed and sparked with electrons, the flashing of silicon synaptic nerves activating latent bootstrap subroutines.

Like a patient awakening from a coma, first aware of light and sound, later self-awareness and recollection, lastly movement and purpose. The machines programs scanned initially for sensory input: light, radio frequencies, background radiation. As more sunlight bathed the solar panels, higher level subroutines kicked in and sought to establish the functioning of each system—motor function, communication, energy. Only when all this had come to pass did the machines finally consider their purpose.

Further into the crater's interior sat a very different machine, a higher order unit. A unit that existed further up the technological evolutionary tree from the humble machines that were now awakening near the crater's edge. It was square and squat at its base, with a large upper structure. On one side, a confusion of communication dishes and antenna protruded. Outwardly, in appearance as least, it was reminiscent of the old Apollo lunar landers. Inside, however, the similarity ended. For one, a small plutonium battery provided energy in abundance, a minuscule portion of which was now being used to call to its servants, the harvester rovers that were awakening after the long 364-hour lunar night. As one by one they responded to their master's call, information on their status was relayed back to anxious eyes on Earth that scrutinized monitors in the Jiuquan Lunar Command and Control Center in Gansu Province, in western China.

Several thousand kilometers away, in the harbor of Port Hercule in Monaco, one of China's leading industrialists, Xiang Zu, also waited for news of the lunar mining project. He sat behind his highly ornate jade inlaid desk on board his opulent super yacht, the Helios.

He was attired only in a pair of oversized red satin boxer shorts with an extremely thick gold chain around his neck. A pair of large black horn-rimmed glasses crowned his bulbous nose, completing the ensemble, and giving him a look not unlike the late Roy Orbison. In front of him on the desk was a Malagasy Giant Chameleon.

Xiang Zu placed his elbows on the desk and rested his chin on clasped hands. He observed the exotic creature with a distracted curiosity. Its strange orbiting eye rotated in his direction.

Feeding time, he thought, as he unclasped his hands and reached down to a lower drawer in the desk, where he removed a small bamboo basket. Opening the lid, he extracted a large green grasshopper, which he then placed in a central position on the desktop. The chameleon's telescopic eye rotated in its direction. Xiang Zu sat back in his chair and waited.

Slap!

In the blink of an eye, the chameleon opened its mouth and unfurled an impossibly long sticky tongue, snagging the dazed grasshopper, then retracted it, leaving only a flailing leg protruding from the side of its mouth. Two bites later, it was gone. Xiang Zu allowed himself the briefest of smiles. He loved feeding time.

Long before the revolution in China ended with the takeover of the country by the communist forces of Mao Zedong in 1949, the Xiang family had ranked among its wealthiest and most prominent industrialists. At that time, the Xiang family businesses were extensive, with interests in mining, engineering, and transport. Xiang Tai, Xiang Zu's grandfather, had profited greatly by war contracts given to him by the Nationalists who were well financed, not least by the Americans. It was rumored that, in total, nearly $3.5 billion had been given in aid by the US before hostilities concluded.

But Marxist China had no room for the capitalists and, one by one, the Xiang family businesses were nationalized until, in 1957, there were no more left. They were now simply citizen workers in Mao's great social experiment. And so it went, until Xiang Tai's fortunes changed in 1978 when the new Chinese leader, Deng Xiaoping, asked him to assist in the redevelopment of China's industry on more market-driven lines.

But Xiang Tai was an old man by this stage, and the task of reestablishing the Xiang family fortunes fell mainly to his oldest son, Xiang Wei, Zu's father. It was he who, having been born into wealth only to experience descent into poverty, was determined to regain those riches a hundredfold. Perhaps it was this deep psychological rent in his being that drove him to acquire ever more wealth. It seemed that no matter what new financial watermark was reached, it was never enough.

By the time Xiang Zu, as his only heir, took over the family empire at the tender age of twenty-four, he instantly became one of the richest men in China and commanded an industrial empire that stretched across all five continents. Yet, for Xiang Zu, this was merely a starting point. In an ever-changing world, it is he who catches and rides the wave of opportunity that ends up on the shores of prosperity, as Xiang Zu would put it.

And so he lost no time in setting about developing his mining interests into precious metals and rare earths to feed the burgeoning demand by consumer technology manufacturers. His aviation industries he developed into drone technology for both military and civilian. But one of his greatest moves was into space technology, specifically in reusable rockets. This made Xiang Industries a direct competitor to Elon Musk's SpaceX. But, more importantly, it made him the go-to contractor for China's increasingly ambitious space program. Unsurprisingly, it was not long after this acquisition that the Chinese state invited Xiang Industries to collaborate on the development of a commercial helium3 fusion reactor. For Xiang Zu, this moment was the most auspicious wave yet to appear on the horizon of his ambition.

Thut...thut...thut...

The sound of a helicopter broke his revere. He fingered a tablet on the side of his desk and brought up a camera view of the helipad on the aft deck. The chopper touched down, whipping up spray as it landed. The side door opened and out stepped Lao Bang, vice-president of Xiang Industries. She was met by his head of security, a man from northern China, of Mongolian descent and noble warrior stock. He possessed a formidable physique, such that most standard furniture had difficulty in accommodating it. At birth, his parents saw fit to bestow upon him a name so phonetically complex that few outside his own clan had the vocal dexterity to satisfactorily pronounce it. As a consequence, he was simply known as Mr. Wang.

Xiang Zu pressed a button on his intercom. "Tell Lao Bang that I will meet her on the operations deck in ten minutes."

By the time he'd reached the opulent operations deck on board the Helios, Lao Bang was busy preparing for the transmission from the Jiuquan Lunar Command and Control Center. The room itself was as opulent as the rest of the vast yacht. One side opened onto a long deck area overlooking the main harbor in Monaco. Other walls were adorned with Oriental paintings and tapestries of varying antiquity.

Lao Bang, a slim and elegant woman in her forties, dressed as always in a tight black suit, her hair a dark bouffant that crowned a leathery face and a pungent cigarette permanently dangling from her lips. She was snapping instructions on her phone as she went to take a seat at the main table. She possessed a razor-sharp mind and an arid dry wit in equal measure.

On his way to the meeting, Xiang Zu had managed to acquire an additional item of clothing. A loud yellow and green Hawaiian shirt. On the back, it had an almost cartoon-like depiction of a flamingo standing on one leg. The same pattern was repeated on the front, but, because it didn't quite meet at the close, the flamingo seemed to possess a dislocated neck.

Lao cast a wry eye in the direction of Xiang Zu and contemplated his eccentric attire. She was never quite sure if his weird and somewhat disconcerting dress sense was simply a ruse to keep everyone else off balance, or if he simply had extremely bad taste. She leaned toward the latter.

"You'll be glad to know we will have a live feed from Guangdau any moment," said Lao Bang.

"Excellent," replied Xiang Zu.

Someone somewhere pressed a button and automatic doors to the balcony closed. The windows dimmed, reducing the ambient light in the room. In tandem with this, the Ming Dynasty tapestry that covered most of the end wall retracted into the celling revealing an array of large monitors. Lao snapped her phone down and announced, "They're ready!"

With that the left monitor flickered to life with a video feed of the Operations Director of the Chinese Command and Control Center. Over his shoulder could be seen an array of technicians sitting at various control desks. The right-hand monitor then relayed a direct feed from the command module on the lunar surface, displaying a bewildering assortment of statistical data. Yet another monitor flickered to life, and a conference connection was set up with Weng Gun, director of the Chinese Communist Party Energy Commission, and Professor Swang Ji, Head of the Experimental Chinese Fusion Reactor Facility in Chengdu, southwest China.

"What's our status?" barked Lao. "All harvester rovers have been in direct sunlight now for over thirty minutes, they should commence operations any moment." The activity down on the control room floor suddenly became more animated as a live video feed materialized on the main screen.

"Patching it through now," came a voice in the background. With that, the central monitor flicked to life, displaying a direct feed from one of the lunar rovers. A gray and desolate terrain stretched off into the distance, pockmarked with the odd rock here and there. In the distance could be seen the silhouette of the central processing module. Beyond that, huge mountains dominated the central crater.

A moment of awe emanated from the assembled members, and Xiang Zu allowed himself the briefest of smiles. *That's twice today,* he thought.

All harvester rovers were now on the move, working autonomously, perambulating laboriously across the lunar surface scooping up soil as they went—not unlike a domestic vacuum robot, with similar simple commands programmed into their silicon brains. *Collect soil until hopper is full, find location of central processing module, go there, unload, repeat ad infinitum.*

And so it begins, thought Xiang Zu, *the second phase of Xiang Industries and China's mission to mine helium3 on the moon.* The first was the launch, two faultless lift-offs eight days apart—one for the rovers and one for the central processing module. The third and final phase would be the return mission, bringing with it glory for the motherland and, more importantly, the promise of an extraordinary fortune for Xiang Zu.

"How long before we know if the operation is successful?" It was Weng Gun, speaking directly to the director of operations at the Command and Control Center. Being a party bureaucrat, he had little knowledge or interest in anything scientific. He was only interested in ensuring that everyone knew he was *The Party.*

"Harvesters will collect soil and return it to the central

processing unit, dumping it into a trough in the base. Once full, it will be conveyed into the processing chamber and heated up to around 780°C. This will release the helium3 gas. We should expect results in a few hours."

"And how long will this process continue?" Weng Gun continued his questioning.

"The rovers are solar powered, and the lunar day is approximately 356 hours, a little over 14 days. We will continue harvesting and processing until then."

"And the return trip?"

"Three days. The helium3 gas released by the processing operation is syphoned off and stored under pressure in the return vehicle sitting on top of the base unit. It will take off in fourteen days' time, three more days for the return trip, so seventeen days approximately until it lands in Mongolia."

"How much do we expect to collect?" It was Professor Swang Ji that spoke now.

"Analysis of the lunar samples returned by the Apollo missions showed helium3 is present over the entire surface of the moon. Also, the data we, eh...acquired from the Indian Chandrayaan-2 orbiter shows a high concentration in this area. If our calculations are correct, then we should expect somewhere around sixty kilograms."

"I see," said Lao Bang, sucking deep on her cigarette and exhaling a voluminous cloud of pungent smoke. "We'll have quadrupled the entire global supply. Impressive."

Onscreen, one of the rovers was now approaching the processing module ready to unload the very first batch of mined lunar soil. It was a seminal moment, a moment savored by all who watched it unfold.

China had long pursued experiments into fusion technology. But, unlike Europe and the US, who had both chosen deuterium and tritium hydrogen isotopes as the fuel of choice, the Chinese had chosen helium3 for the reaction. Using hydrogen makes a lot of sense since it's the most plentiful element on Earth. Water is two-thirds hydrogen and Earth is two-thirds water. In terms of quantity, it was, for all intents and purposes, limitless. However, using hydrogen requires an extremely complex, and hence a potentially unreliable, reactor.

The upside for the Chinese choice of helium3 is that they required a simpler design of reactor. It meant very little fuel was required as it produced a much more efficient reaction, with little or no radioactivity. The downside, however, was that unlike hydrogen, helium3 was almost nonexistent on Earth. So rare, in fact, that it could only be acquired as a by-product from the decommissioning of nuclear weapons. The entire global stockpile of helium3 consisted of a mere 19 kilograms—and that was controlled by the Americans. The Moon, on the other hand, had helium3 in abundance.

"Professor, can you give us an update on the development of the fusion reactor?" said Lao Bang.

"The reactor is complete, and we have had excellent results with our initial stockpile, but we are still several months away from producing a self-sustaining reaction."

"And how confident are you that it will succeed?"

"We are very close. Now that we have an abundant supply of fuel, we see no other obstacles in our path."

There was a momentary silence as the group considered this information and its relevance.

"Does all this really matter?" said Weng Gun shaking his head. "Tomorrow, ITER goes live and the Europeans will have won the race. We all know what that means. If they are successful in their ignition test there will be two competing technologies, and they have a head start. Not good for business."

"You're assuming they will succeed," said Lao Bang. "Remember what happened to the American reactor at Livermore last year."

The Party Director chuckled. "Ha ha, yes. That was most unfortunate."

"With that, gentlemen, I must conclude our discussions and leave you," Xiang Zu interjected. "There's still much work to done."

They signed off and the conference feed terminated.

Xiang Zu turned to Lao Bang. "Did you bring the, eh... device for Mr. Wang?"

"Yes, he's instructing Marcel as to its function as we speak. Marcel will be overseeing the handover operation this morning in Saint-Raphael, and the final component should be in place later today."

"Excellent, excellent." Xiang Zu leaned back in his chair allowed himself the faintest of smiles.

Three today. He was positively giddy.

5

CROSSING

Marcel considered his reflection in the mirror as he unconsciously fingered the worn wooden cross that he wore around his neck—it was a habit of his. In moments of uncertainty, his hand would move reflexively to the small cross. It gave him solace. He had made it himself when he was just a child, carved from some old rosewood one of the monks at Tibhirine had pruned from the monastery garden. He had been so proud of it that he ran straight to the abbot and showed him his childish work. The abbot had smiled a broad smile as he looked at it. "Marcel, why, this is beautiful." Then he knelt down in front of him and tied it around his neck with a leather string, and, from that day to this, he had never taken it off. That was a long time ago now.

Marika was dead, lying at the bottom of the Mediterranean wrapped in heavy chain with a bullet through her head, and there was nothing Marcel could do about it. They said she was a spy, a French Intelligence agent, and he was a *schmuck*, fooled by her charms, by late night pillow-talk and a tender caress. Poor dumb Marcel. He punched the wall beside the mirror, leaving a dent in the woodwork and blood on his knuckles. "Shit." He held his hand as the physical pain began to register and push aside his emotional turmoil. "Shit, shit, shit."

Maybe he could have saved her, but he didn't. "She was using you. She didn't really love you," he said to himself. "Why am I so stupid. I can't make sense of it."

A vision of her terror, just before Xiang Zu shot her, was burned into his memory. It was a look he had seen many times on many faces. A look of terrified resignation. The moment when the victim knows they're going to die. But those were people he didn't care about. It's easier to put a bullet in someone's brain when you just don't give a shit. It's just a job.

It was Xiang Zu who had made him this way. He remembered that fateful day, over a decade ago now, when he was just a boy. Xiang Zu plucked him off the filth ridden alleyways of Algiers and gave him a life. He took him in and made him what he is today. *And what am I today?* he thought. *I know I'm not the man I was yesterday.*

Tap, tap!

Marcel flinched and looked at his watch. Who the hell was knocking at his cabin at this time? He opened the door a cautious crack. Standing in the corridor was Sofia du Maurier, one of the cabin crew of the Helios.

"Sofia, what is it?"

"Marcel, have you seen Marika?"

Crap, thought Marcel. *This is all I need.* "She left last night, after we'd docked." His voice was calm.

"Oh, she never told anyone she was going. Are you sure?"

"Yes, I'm sure." Marcel nodded.

"I tried calling her, but she didn't answer her phone. I hope she's alright."

Marcel tried to calm the storm that was building inside him. "She's fine. She just got another gig, or something."

Sofia didn't seem convinced. "Maybe I should ask Mr. Wang."

Marcel stepped out and grabbed her gently by the arm. He looked up and down the corridor.

"Listen, do yourself a favor and drop it, okay?"

Sofia looked perplexed and a little frightened.

"Mr. Wang is, eh...a bit pissed off with her for leaving like that, you know. So I wouldn't go asking about her or you might be looking for a new gig yourself. You know what he's like."

"Okay, sure, Marcel." She backed away meekly.

He turned, went back inside and closed the door. Sofia had better keep her mouth shut, or she would be next for a watery grave. He sat down on the edge of his bunk and took a small leather-bound diary out of his pocket and looked at it. His mind went back to the previous night in Marika's cabin, after he was ordered to cleared out her shit.

Mr. Wang had exposed her treachery, and Xiang Zu eliminated her. But Marcel was the one who felt most betrayed. After the body was disposed of, he gladly accepted the job to eradicate all trace of her from the Helios. On his way to her cabin, he had brought some large carryall bags weighed down with heavy chain. He opened wardrobes and drawers and shoved everything he could find into the bags. Finally, he broke open a locked drawer in the table beside her bed. Inside was a leather-bound diary. He opened it but had difficulty reading her stylized, flowing calligraphy. Tucked in the back was a handwritten letter and inside it was an old photograph of a peasant couple, happily smiling with a baby girl sitting between them.

She was French Algerian, just like himself. Perhaps that's why they'd come together. Her parents were peasant farmers in Hauts Plateaux in northern Algeria. But she had beauty and intelligence and a burning desire to get out of grinding poverty by any means possible. Or, at least, so her story went. She had come on board a few months earlier with some other crew. He didn't know what she did, she simply said *research*. Others said she was just a whore.

Their liaisons had been tentative at first, and secret, at her request—now he understood. He had had lots of other women in the past, but she was different. Marika touched places that Marcel didn't know he had. She opened hidden doors in his soul and exposed the dormant emotions within: fear, loneliness and love.

His own mother had been a prostitute in Algiers, working the streets, poor, hungry, dangerous. It was one night when the monks of Tibhirine were doing their rounds of the Christian quarter that they found her, battered, bloody, and dying on the side of an alley. They took her in and nursed her back to life. They gave her a chance. It was four months later that Marcel was born, in the shadow of the monastery Notre-Dame de l'Atlas of Tibhirine. He lived there until he was fourteen, then he ran away, out into the big, bad world.

Marcel clutched the wooden cross around his neck and did something he had never done since he was a child—he wept: for himself, for Marika, for his mother, for the monks who gave him a chance, for the shit he had taken, for the shit he had given, and for all the shit in this shit fucking world—he wept.

Eventually, he stood up, wiped his face, and put the diary with the letter in his pocket. The rest of the contents of the drawer he put in the bags and headed out of her cabin. Once up on deck, he flung the bags overboard. He stood there for a while and watched them sink into the depths of the Mediterranean Sea.

That was last night, now he had more important work to do, a mission for Xiang Zu. He needed to be strong, not show his emotions, not reveal his inner turmoil to his master. Inside, he felt that this job may be his last, but he shook the thought away, took a deep breath, and straightened himself up. He had heard the helicopter arriving earlier bringing Lao Bang. It was time to go.

He opened the door of his cabin and stepped out onto the long walkway. At the far end, he descended the stairwell heading for the lower decks. As he walked through the crew accommodation deck, he passed Marika's cabin. He slowed and stopped to look at the door. He gripped the railing tight and suppressed the emotion that was fermenting inside him. He forced himself to move on, and the turmoil subsided. Eventually he passed above the engine room and entered a huge area at the stern of the boat, housing all manner of vehicles. On one side sat the one of the ship's tenders along with several powerful rigid inflatables.

Marcel checked his watch. *Where is that Mongolian monster?* he wondered. With that, Mr. Wang stepped out from behind a boat at the very far end of the massive marine garage and signaled to Marcel to come over. He then unfastened a complex looking diver's watch from his left wrist and placed it carefully on a clean workbench.

Marcel glanced down at the watch. "Is that it?"

"What where you expecting? A bomb in a suitcase?" Mr. Wang replied with a smirk.

"I don't know. It just looks so small." Marcel shook his head in wonder.

"Trust me, it is more than adequate to do the job. Now pay attention while I explain it to you." Mr. Wang then proceeded to go through its setup and operation several times. When he had finished, he made Marcel repeat it back so he fully understood the device's function as well as all the details of the mission. Finally, he handed it over to him. "Don't screw this up."

Marcel strapped the device to his wrist, nodded to Mr. Wang, and walked off to find Nikolai, one of the ships mechanics. He found him over in the workshop area fiddling with an outboard engine.

"Nikolai, I need a bike."

The burly Russian lifted his head out of the engine and wiped his hands on a cloth. "Okay, okay." He loped over to a desk and grabbed a set of keys from one of the drawers. "Here you go, and don't fucking bend it. I'm sick of fixing your shit."

Marcel ignored him, grabbed a helmet, straddled one of the bikes—a Ducati Multistrada—and started it up.

As Marcel waited for the Russian to open the stern bay doors, he reached into his pocket and took out Marika's diary, just to feel it again, the soft leather. The beauty of it drew him in like a spell. He clasped it to his chest, against the cross around his neck, and tried to hold his emotions in check. Just then, the bay doors cracked open, and a flood of sunlight broke over Marcel, like a sign from the heavens.

"Hey, Marcel, who are you praying to? The great hooker in the sky? Ha ha. Is that Marika one not letting you into her locker room?"

Marcel dismounted the bike and walked over to Nikolai, putting the diary back in his pocket as he strode. Nikolai was still holding the button for the doors when Marcel slammed his head into the bulkhead, and down he went like a wet sponge. He came up again, holding the side of his face.

Marcel grabbed his hair and yanked his head back. With his other hand he reached into his pocket and took out an old Zippo lighter. He held it in front of Nikolai's face.

"Jesus, Marcel...it was just a joke, man...a joke."

"Do you see this lighter?"

"Christ sakes, Marcel."

Marcel yanked his head back further.

"Yes, yes. I see it."

With one dexterous thumb, Marcel flipped the lid and lit it. "Say another word about Marika and I will burn your testicles off, one by one with this lighter." For emphasis, he brought it close to Nikolai's face and let it singe his nasal hairs.

"Okay, okay, sure, Marcel. Jesus Christ, man."

Marcel snapped the lighter closed, walked back to his bike and fired it up again. *Goddamn Russians,* he thought. He put on his helmet again and drove out the stern bay doors, up the ramp, and onto the promenade heading out of Monaco for the A8 to the port of Saint-Raphael. This was going to be his last mission—he knew it in his heart.

6

WAKEUP CALL

Marcel sipped a mug of hot coffee in the kitchen of a spacious, modern apartment in the center of the French town of Saint-Raphael. He then took out his phone and sent a text message.

I'm in your kitchen. BTW your coffee is shit.

A few seconds later, he heard a ping from a phone a few meters away, behind one of the bedroom doors. A few seconds after that, a confused and irate Imran Dhaliwal, senior programmer at ITER, peered around the kitchen door, uncertain of what to expect. He was holding a cricket bat in one hand, ready to use it as a weapon.

When he saw Marcel, he relaxed. "For God's sakes, Marcel, why can't you use the door buzzer like a normal human?"

"Your security is very poor, it's easier just to walk in. Playing cricket today, are we?"

Imran put down the bat and sat at the table. Marcel pushed a mug of coffee across to him. He took a sip. "Did you bring it?" he asked.

Marcel straddled a kitchen chair, unstrapped the device from his wrist, and placed it on the table. Imran picked it up and examined it. It looked like a standard analogue diver's watch. "Clever," he said. "Simple, but clever."

Employees at ITER were not allowed to bring any electronic devices into the control room zone. No smartphones, tablets, USB sticks—nothing. Such was the data security surrounding the facility that anyone caught meant disciplinary action, even dismissal. But an analog watch, who would think of that? Very simple. He put it back down on the table and took another sip of coffee. "So how does it work?"

Marcel rotated the serrated dial around the face of the watch and pressed one of the buttons on the side. The back then detached from the face, essentially making two separate devices. The front part with one strap attached, and the back with the other strap. He lifted one up and peeled away a strip at the back of the strap to reveal a tiny optical cable splicer.

"This one is to be attached to the optical data cable on the ITER control side." He flipped over the other one and did the same. "This one goes onto any of the data cables coming in from the outside world. Once they're in place, you need to activate them by entering this code using the dial on the front, just like on a safe." Marcel handed him a small card with the activation code on it.

Imran picked up one of the devices and examined it with

awe. It was like some sort of alien technology, exotic and dangerous. "A data bridge, very bloody clever."

The ITER systems were physically isolated from the outside world, so there was no way they could be hacked into and the data stolen. But there was still a data pipe to the world for other systems in ITER, the less important ones for email, conferencing, and whatnot. These devices created a data bridge and allowed access to CODAC, the central control system interfacing with all ITER reactor systems, including those for safety and shutdown.

"That's quite a knockoff your Chinese friends made." He put the device back on the table. "Okay, that's great, but where's my money?"

"Check your account," said Marcel as he sat back and lit up a cigarette.

"Hey, no smoking here."

"Go screw yourself, fat man," said Marcel, and he blew a stream of smoke in Imran's face.

Imran coughed and waved his arms around, then rose from the table and sidled off into the main living room to check his new offshore account. A moment later he returned—a broad smile on his face.

"Happy?" asked Marcel.

"One million dollars, who wouldn't be," replied Imran.

"You'll get the other half when the job is done." Marcel rose from the table and headed out. "Make sure it's done today, otherwise you're a dead fat man, okay?" He poked Imran hard in his ample belly.

"It will, just make sure the balance gets paid," said Imran by way of a feeble retort.

Marcel stalled, scratched his chin, and then his hand went to the cross around his neck. He turned back to Imran and considered him for a moment. "Do yourself a favor, Imran. After you've planted the device, get out fast, don't hang around here too long." He spoke almost in a whisper.

"Why, what's the problem?"

"Just do it. Okay?"

"Hey, believe me, I don't intend to be here one second longer than I have to."

Marcel nodded, turned, and walked out the door, still clutching the cross.

7

NO PEOPLE

A thin filament of acrid smoke corkscrewed from the underside of an electronic circuit board as Charles Gardner applied the tip of a soldering iron to a silvery connection. He was seated in the cramped confines of a small workshop he had fashioned in the port cabin of his sailboat, and was currently immersed in the process of fixing a faulty solar inverter that had been giving him trouble all the way since Genoa.

Cheap crap, he thought. *I should have invested in something better.* He flipped the board over and began checking the integrity of the components when he felt the familiar rock of the boat as someone stepped on board. He spun around on his workshop stool and headed up top to investigate.

The morning sun was directly astern the boat, blinding him as he emerged from the dim environment of his cabin workshop. He held a hand up to protect his vision and tried to make out the form that was now materializing out of the incandescent brightness.

An ethereal being took shape... an angel with a brilliant halo framing her golden hair... a white translucent garment enveloped her body. But as his eyes began to adjust, the translucent garment became a light linen suit... with a badge... a customs official badge. "Mr. Gardner?"

"Uh... yes?" Charles rubbed his eyes.

"Are you Charles Gardner?"

"Yes, that's me."

"I'm Inspector Madelaine Duchamp of the Monaco Harbor Police, and we are doing a standard customs check. We would like to take a look around your boat."

Charles stood mute, like a deer in the headlights. Here was the very person he had called to report the murder. Yet he had gone out of his way to hide his identity. There was absolutely no way she could know it was him, just no way. *This has to be a coincidence,* he thought. *It's simply a random customs check. It happens all the time at every port. Just keep cool.*

"Mr. Gardner?"

"Yes...of course...of course." His hand still shaded his squinting eyes as if he were afraid to look straight at her. He much preferred her as a translucent celestial being rather than an officious police inspector.

Three uniformed officers who had been waiting on the boardwalk now hopped on board and began poking around. One was wearing a digital lens over one eye, a tell-tail red light blinking. *Realtime video analysis, augmented reality overlay,* Charles considered. He imagined the read-out, all his details being displayed to the wearer—name, nationality, and God knows what else. No place to hide any more, no place to be alone, everyone reduced to a data stream. Soon, to have no data trail and be off-grid would be a good enough reason for suspicion.

Another officer began marshaling a dog on to the boat, a lively looking Golden Labrador. *A dope dog,* Charles presumed. At least here was a technology that had been around for a very long time. Even in this 21st century, there was still no gadget that could replace the wonders of the canine schnozzle.

"Could I see your passport, Mr. Gardner?"

"Eh, sure. It's down below, this way." He gestured toward the salon and began to descend the companionway steps into the soothing dimness of the yacht interior. Inspector Madelaine Duchamp followed. Charles made his way to his cabin at the bow of the boat where he kept his passport in a safe built under the bunk. He heard the dog scrabbling around up top, sniffing and panting hard in the heat of the day.

When he reemerged, the inspector was standing looking a one of his watercolor paintings, of which he had many mounted along the walls of the yacht interior. She turned around and accepted the passport, giving it a cursory look, her eyes flicking from it to her tablet screen. She then looked back at another of his paintings. This one was of a lighthouse, the ancient Venetian lighthouse in the old town of Chania on the island of Crete. He had sketched it one afternoon sitting at one of the many cafés dotted along the harbor earlier on this trip. That seemed like a long time ago now.

Lighthouses are such noble constructions, he thought, *built to withstand everything the elements could throw at them. Standing tall and proud in the midst of the maelstrom, majestic and immutable, their light both a comfort and a warning to the mariner out at sea. They are the difference between safe passage or grounded wreck, of making harbor or lost at sea, the difference between life and death. They are Neptune's sentinels, aloof and immortal.*

"Are you a painter, Mr. Gardner?" The inspector gave him a curious look.

"Mr. Gardner?" she prompted again.

"Uh..." His mind returned. "Oh, I just dabble."

"Dabble?"

Charles considered this question. Having spent over twenty years in the electronic surveillance business, Charles had worked with enough cops to spot a standard ploy used to get a person talking without saying anything yourself. And that was to repeat the last word of every sentence. It goes something like this.

"So, Mr. Jones, where were you on the night of the 5th?"

"I was at home watching TV."

"TV?"

"Yes, with my girlfriend."

"Girlfriend?"

"Say, leave her out of this, she had nothing to do with it."

At which point the perp realizes he's just walked right into it. However, just like the Jedi mind control trick, it only works on the dimwitted. So, there are a number of escape routes, one of which is to play them at their own game.

"Dabble!" he said. *Now she's in check, your move,* he thought.

She consulted her tablet again, presumably a tactic to avoid conceding defeat in her initial line of questioning. "Are you traveling on your own?"

"Yes."

"Staying long?"

"No, just a few days, until after the Fusion Conference here in Monaco."

"Are you attending?"

"No, I'm meeting my daughter here, she's flying in from London for the conference. She's a science journalist. She's covering it for a major TV channel. That's why I'm here... to meet her."

One of the other customs officers then stuck his head in the cockpit door and said something in French that Charles couldn't quite catch, sounded like *termites*. Madelaine waved her hand, he nodded back, and left. Looks like he wasn't being searched after all. Just a cover to ask a few questions perhaps?

She returned to gazing at the paintings. "You're very good, Mr. Gardner."

"Pardon?"

"Your paintings, they're very good."

"Oh, thanks."

"You said you came in last night ahead of the storm."

"Yeah."

"Much traffic?"

"A few dots here and there on the radar."

"Did you notice anything unusual while you were sailing in?"

And there it is, he thought. She was fishing, on the hunt. His phone call had had the desired effect, or so it seemed, only why was she interrogating him? There was just no way she could know it was him that phoned. Then it struck him. *She's talking to all the boats that came in last night.*

"No, nothing out of the ordinary."

She looked at him, the way all detectives the world over look at you, deep into your soul. A look that says, *I know you are lying through your teeth, I know you committed a most heinous crime and I'm going to hunt you down to the ends of the earth and put you away for all eternity, so you might as well confess now and save us all the bother.*

Charles returned her stare and held it there.

"Well, I think we're done here," she said with a flourish. The inspector wandered back toward the companionway and then spotted the open workshop door. She peered inside. The small cabin was floor to ceiling with boxes and drawers of boat chandlery, electronic components, engine parts, hand tools, and a plethora of other flotsam and jetsam all neatly sorted, labeled, and stacked.

"That's quite a little workshop you have there."

"Yes, thanks. Always something to fix on a boat." He gave her a smile.

"Very organized, are you an engineer?"

"Yes...well, I was...I mean, I'm retired. Electronic engineer. I had a security electronics business for a long time." There he goes again, he thought. He kept saying more than was necessary. But what the hell did he have to hide? After all, he wasn't the criminal. And she was just doing her job, the job he had hoped she'd be doing.

"Is an engineer something you can retire from?"

Charles laughed and thought about this. She had a point. "Ha, yes, I see what you mean, perhaps not."

She turned and was about to head up the companionway steps when she stopped to gaze at another one of his sketches.

"No people," she said, her eyes fixed on the sketch.

"Eh... sorry?"

"Your paintings, they have no people in them."

Charles looked at the sketch. He'd never noticed this before, even though he had painted and sketched them all. She was right. They were of lighthouses, harbors, beaches, boats, landscapes. None had people in them. He wondered what that meant. Did it mean anything? Maybe it meant he wasn't very good at painting people.

"By the way"—she was now up top and peering down through the hatch at Charles—"if you do remember anything unusual from last night, you can contact me here." She handed him a card.

He took it and gave it a brief look. "Oh, okay, sure."

"Enjoy your stay, Mr. Gardner," and she was gone.

Charles wandered over to the galley and sat down at the table. He looked at the card. *Detective Inspector Madelaine Duchamp, Monaco Harbor Police.*

44

Well, at least he hadn't given much away, just that that he was a retired security electronics engineer meeting his scientist daughter who was covering the Fusion Conference for a major TV channel. It also struck him that he should never contemplate embarking on a career as a criminal since he would be a complete failure at it.

After some time, he decided that the entire encounter distilled down to one fundamental question. Was the inspector investigating a murder, or was she looking to apprehend a crank caller who was possibly unhinged and therefore a threat to the safety of the great and the good of Monaco? The answer, in Charles's mind, was far from certain. He looked over at one of his paintings. *No people,* he mused, *what the hell did that mean anyway?*

He thought about getting back to his workshop and fixing the solar inverter, but his mind wasn't on it. Instead, he turned and plucked a bottle of ten-year-old, single malt, Irish whiskey out of a salon locker, cracked the cap, and poured himself two fingers. He was just plonking a few ice cubes into his glass when his pocket vibrated. He fished his phone out and looked at the screen. It was his daughter, Leonie. He answered.

"Hi, where are you?"

"At Heathrow. The plane leaves in an hour. Oh my god, it was such a panic to get here, been chasing my tail all day, so many things to organize, you would swear I was on a mission to a war zone the way the channel is going on about it." She let out a big sigh. "Anyway... how are you?"

"Good, I'm in Monaco, got in last night."

"Great, I should be there in a few hours, we're flying into Nice."

"Do you need a lift? I've still got my bike."

"No dad, you're not getting me on that thing. It's fine, we have a car waiting for us, lots of equipment to carry, the usual TV stuff. Hopefully David and Kats remembered to bring everything this time, not like that time in Cern. David forgot the chargers, kept saying Kats was bringing them. Laurel and bloody Hardy."

"Okay, no worries. It would be hard getting all that stuff on my bike."

"Yeah, for sure. Anyway, just to let you know I'm on my way and I'll give you a ping when I'm in Monte Carlo. By the way, I got you a present."

"Wow, thanks. What is it?"

"Oh... can't tell you that yet. It's a surprise."

"A surprise, eh?"

"A little surprise."

"Great, I can't wait."

"I'll see you soon, love you."

"I love you too."

"Bye."

He put the phone down on the table, took a sip of whiskey, and into his mind flashed an image of the woman from the previous night. The woman who was now dead. She was someone's daughter, too. Maybe there was a father out there somewhere who would never hear her voice again, would never hear her say *I love you*, would never know what had happened to his *little girl*, he would wait and wait, for the rest of his life—and would never know.

He had a few hours before Leonie arrived, so he considered it might time to visit the natives and try his hand at painting people. He gathered together some bits and pieces into a rucksack, downed the rest of the whiskey, and headed out the cabin door. As he stepped on to the marina boardwalk, he took his phone out of his pocket and thumbed his way to his security app and set it to *arm*. The boat was now locked up tight. Any incursion would be reported to him instantly. *Can never be too careful,* he thought. *Even here in the safest little country on the planet.*

At Route del la Piscine he turned on to the main backbone of the harbor and out to where the largest of the super yachts were moored. He sat on a low wall, unpacked a battered sketch pad from his rucksack, and contemplated the scene before him. By now the sun had reached its zenith, and by rights the intense heat of the day should have put most sensible people into maintenance mode, but this was Monaco. While inside the wealthy cooled in the comfort of their air-conditioned floating mansions, outside the tourists gawked and clicked as the delivery vans restocked the pantries of the pampered.

Charles reached into his rucksack and selected an HB pencil as his weapon of choice. It had a lead that was not too hard and not too soft. He began to apply the first strokes to the paper. These were always the main constructs of the sketch, the initial foundation lines, essential to get the broad form blocked out. He squinted his eyes and looked at the subject matter. This was a trick he had learnt over time. Most beginners will try to draw literally what they see, but by squinting one's eyes, the focus becomes blurred and all you can really make out is the form in blocks of light and dark.

In the bright Mediterranean sun, colors become rich and vivid. The landscape illuminates with the bright blues of the sea, the burnt reds of the earth, and the verdant greens of the vegetation. A kaleidoscopic mosaic all bound by stark shadows and brilliant light. For those who painted in the muted pallet of the northern hemisphere, the light of the south of France was both a panacea and a beacon. Many of the great painters of the early 20th century flocked to the Cote d'Azur to seek out its fabled *luminosity*. Matisse, Signac, even Picasso. Like moths around the lamp, they flocked to the south and made it the playground of the bohemian decadent, later the glamorous fashionista and, ultimately, the wealthy socialite.

By now, Charles had sketched out the main focus of his harbor scene, which mostly included the stern of the super yacht, the Helios. He had positioned himself in such a way at the busy port so he could get a clear view of the boat and, from this vantage point, he could see all the comings and goings around the aft of the luxury yacht. He wondered if the CIA had ever contemplated using landscape painters as spies since it seemed to him that you could spend all day looking at something without raising any suspicion whatsoever. Just another painter dude doing his thing.

During the hour or so he had spent so far, he had seen precious little activity. He began to wonder why he was even doing this, spying on the Helios. What could he hope to achieve? Perhaps it was just a morbid curiosity, that same primal compulsion that makes people slow down at a car crash, hoping to catch a glimpse of the carnage, or that which drives the criminal back to the scene of the crime.

His musings were interrupted by a shadow that crossed his peripheral vision and came to rest over his painting. The shadow also came with a waft of pungent cigarette smoke. Someone was standing behind him having a look at his efforts. Charles was used to this, lots of people would see an artist at work and stop to have a look. Some would utter a word or two of praise. Most would simply walk on, perhaps judging it unworthy of comment.

"Your painting is very good," said a voice behind him.

"Thanks," said Charles, not caring to look around.

"I would love to buy it from you, would you sell it?"

Charles turned. It was an Asian woman, strangely attired with a black cigarette clamped between her lips. Beside her were two bodyguards, eyes darting this way and that. He half expected them to start talking into their cuffs.

Charles thought about this for a moment. Normally he didn't sell his paintings, he tended to give them away to friends and family. He looked back at the painting. What did he want this for anyway? He was never going to hang it up, it would only serve to remind him of an event he would rather forget. At that instant he realized the folly of what he was doing. Maybe he had spent too long at sea on his own. Maybe he was losing his grip on reality.

"If you like it, you can have it—for free," he said, turning to the woman.

"Really? That's very generous of you. Thank you."

"Don't mention it. Paintings are meant to be seen, not stuck in a dusty folder somewhere."

"Very true."

Charles looked back at the painting. "I'm not finished it, though. I still have a few touch ups to do."

"Maybe you could drop it in to me on the boat, or I could have someone call back in a while?"

"No, it's no problem, I'll drop it in to you. Which boat are you on?"

"Why, the one in the painting, of course. I was thinking it would make an interesting present for the owner."

Charles froze. *Holy crap,* he thought. What was he getting himself into?

"Sure... later..." he managed to stammer.

With that she presented him with her card. "Just ask for me, and thank you again." She bowed to him and walked on, her bodyguards following. Charles watched her go, heading up the gangplank and onto the stern of the Helios. She turned, caught his eye, and waved. He waved back.

That was it, he decided, enough was enough. He packed up his bag and headed away from the main harbor, back to the sanity of his own boat. *Enough of this CIA shit*, he thought.

8

THE SUPERIOR MAN

Alone in the operations room on board the Helios, Xiang Zu observed the lunar rovers' silent mechanical ballet. He did so with a hypnotic fascination as they harvested soil and returned it to the factory module—over and over again, like an ant colony endlessly foraging with an unfailing rhythm.

He poured himself some tea from a delicate china teapot and took a sip. The antique set depicted a pastoral scene of Confucius teaching his apprentice under the shade of a cherry blossom, and Xiang Zu's mind went to Marcel, his wayward security agent.

Every scholar should have a student, he considered. A disciple if you will, and Marcel was his. One a fateful day, well over a decade ago now, he had plucked him out of the gutter in Algiers and, in an act of almost reckless benevolence, had taken him to his bosom.

Back then, Marcel was rough and ragged; nonetheless, he did possess a natural proclivity for violence—it was his talent. So, Xiang Zu, the master, administered enlightenment and Marcel, the student, grew and blossomed. But that was then. What troubled Xiang Zu of late was that the apprentice was beginning to question his teaching, question even his purpose. Perhaps his scholarly experiment needed to be terminated. Although Marcel was currently on a mission of some importance, he considered that perhaps this should be his last.

Yet Marcel was not his main concern—it was more of an irritant, like an itch that needed scratching. Now that the lunar operation to mine helium3 was up and running, and the fly in the ointment that was the French agent Marika had been dealt with, his mind was now consumed by one thing and one thing only—ITER. Should they succeed in their quest to produce a sustainable fusion reaction, it would seriously undermine the commercial viability of Xiang Industries' alternative helium3 reactor. But he had been planning this for a very long time, there was just one more move on the board and he could then ride that wave of opportunity all the way to the shore.

An alert pinged from a small tablet computer on his desk. He tapped the icon and a video link expanded on the main screen. It was Lao Bang.

"We've got word that the Harbor Police are planning a customs search."

Xiang Zu cocked an eyebrow in response.

"It would seem that last night's activities did not go unnoticed," continued Lao Bang.

"It's just coincidence," Xiang Zu said dismissively, sipping his tea.

"When have we ever been searched in Monaco? It just doesn't happen." Lao Bang was not convinced.

"I agree it's somewhat of an imposition, but aren't you being just a little melodramatic?"

"Maybe. Anyway, they'll be here in a few minutes. I'll be up on the lido deck." She signed off.

Xiang Zu took a final sip of tea, sighed, and made his way to the upper deck of the luxury yacht. This was the largest entertaining area, with a sumptuous Italian classical interior sweeping out onto a sprawling sun deck. At the far end, Lao Bang was leaning against the railing looking out over the harbor of Monte Carlo, a pungent cigarette dangling from her lips. She was bookended by her two ever-present bodyguards.

Xiang Zu sidled over beside her.

"Are you sure about this intel?" he asked, sounding skeptical.

By way of an answer, Lao Bang pointed down to the stern of the boat. A Monaco Harbor Customs official was embarking followed by five uniformed officers and a dog.

Xiang Zu took a moment to consider this incursion into his private domain and what it might mean. Perhaps it was someone new, someone who did not know the way things ran in Monaco, someone who was very shortly going to lose their job. Nevertheless, there was nothing he could do right now. He would have to let them come on board and suck it up.

They watched from the vantage point of the upper sun deck as the officers fanned out in different directions. The official in charge seemed very interested in the stern, examining it, looking over and down along the side of the hull, all the time being carefully shadowed by the ever-vigilant Mr. Wang, who was busy fielding her queries. After some time, she spoke into the VHF radio that she held and the other officers drifted back one by one. Then, after a brief discussion with Mr. Wang, they all filed off the boat like a line of toy soldiers.

"Find out who she is," said Xiang Zu as he headed back to the operations room. It was time to phone a friend.

9

THE PATRIOT

Moshe Levy, an Israeli drone operations expert par excellence currently in the employ of Xiang Zu, was regarded as a legend. Stories of his exploits were legendary, so much so that he had been nicknamed *The Patriot*.

One such story concerned an incident only nine months previous. A situation had occurred in the ass-end of Mauritania, a desperately poor desert nation in northwestern Africa, riven by war, famine, and unstable government. Nevertheless, it did possess considerable natural resources of which Xiang Industries had a number of copper mining concessions. However, Amadou Bengazi, the local warlord controlling one of the most valuable regions, suddenly discovered religious fervor. God came to him in a dream one night and chastised him for fraternizing with the oriental infidel. The upshot of this was his withdrawal of support for the mineral exploration program being conducted by Xiang Industries in the region that he controlled. Several attempts at discussion and negotiation came to naught, so the decision was made—he needed to be taken out.

The compound of Amadou Bengazi was just outside the small town of Akjoujt and was well protected with about twenty or so armed guards. Marcel's idea was a stealth attack under cover of darkness with no more than four operatives. Two would take out the perimeter guards with suppressed sniper fire, two others would smoke out any off-duty guards in the bunk house with CS gas and hit them when they evacuated. They would then hook up and all four would enter the main house and take out anyone inside with a shit load of automatic weapons fire and the odd grenade, if necessary. It was an eminently sensible plan with a high potential for success.

But no—The Patriot had a better idea. Fundamentally, Marcel was a 20th-century man in his thinking, whereas The Patriot, on the other hand, was very much 21st century. His plan was simple. From the relative comfort of the Xiang Industries facility in the center of Akjoujt, he sent out one of his tiny insect *death drones* late one night. Through the window it went, guided by preset GPS coordinates, and wafted its way autonomously toward the target. Then under the control of The Patriot's deft hand it entered the compound and flew low around the oblivious guards and into the main house through an open window. Half an hour later, The Patriot gave it the instruction to return, and promptly went to bed. Marcel had watched all this on screen and, to his untrained eye, nothing seemed to have happened other than simple surveillance.

But, two days later, news reports began to mention the mysterious death of Amadou Bengazi and his entire camp. Speculation as to the cause of death ranged from witchcraft to God's wrath to food poisoning. It was only after the autopsy report, nearly three weeks later, that it was concluded that cause of death was asphyxiation due to a lethal dose of curare, a deadly botanical toxin that kills by paralyzing every muscle of the body except the heart. You die because you can't breathe. This was just one story of The Patriot's exploits. There were many others.

In the security control room on board the Helios, The Patriot's fingers danced across a keyboard as a video feed expanded on the primary monitor screen. It was a recording from the ship's security cameras during the customs search.

"Inspector Madelaine Duchamp," said The Patriot, as he pushed his wire-framed glasses back up on his nose and pointed at the image on the monitor. "The interesting thing— assuming our sources are correct—is that she received an anonymous call this morning from someone who claims to have witnessed the French agent getting dispatched last night. We understand the call came in from Nice."

"That's not possible," said an incredulous Mr. Wang, who's eyes were now fixed in the image of the inspector. "We were out in the middle of the sea, miles from the coast."

Again, The Patriot's fingers danced across his keyboard and a new image expanded on screen. He swung around in his chair and looked at Mr. Wang. "Now pay attention, my Mongolian friend, this next bit is important. What you are looking at is a time-lapse of the ship's radar around the time last night when our French problem was dealt with. You see that blip there?" He pointed to a tiny dot of illumination on the screen. "Well, that's a small boat, about half a mile off our stern. Now watch how it moves over that period."

The blip moved toward them for a short time, then suddenly turned southeast for a while, then north.

"So what are you trying to show me here?" said Mr. Wang.

The Patriot gave an exasperated sigh. "This blip is most likely a small yacht, judging by the way it's moving—see, it's tacking as it sails into the wind. Look here."

The time-lapse now showed the blip following a zig-zag course. "However, prior to that, it was on a direct course and easy sail, until it comes to within around a quarter mile off our stern. Then it changes course, not just enough to avoid hitting up, but one that puts distance between it and us. The curious this is that this occurred at exactly the same time as Marika was being dispatched." The Patriot pointed at a time stamp on the recording.

"So, the question is, did someone on that boat see something they shouldn't have?" He pushed his glasses up again and looked over at Mr. Wang.

Mr. Wang remained silent for a while, eyes fixed on the radar image. "Do you know where it went?" he finally said.

The Patriot shook his head. "Not specifically. But, judging by its original course, and taking into consideration that there was a storm brewing at the time, I would guess it was heading for safe harbor somewhere here in Monaco. Or possibly just outside the border in Cap d'Ail."

"Hmmm, not much to go on." Mr. Wang scratched his chin, thinking. "Okay, first things first. We need to keep an eye on the inspector, see where she goes, who she talks to."

"That sounds like a job for my *little friends*. Allow me to introduce you." The Patriot reached under his desk and pressed a hidden switch.

A section of the wooden inlay on the surface of the desk split apart to expose a digital keypad and fingerprint scanner. He then swiped his index finger and punched in some numbers. A faint humming sound emanated from within the security room as the desk and part of the wall behind slid gently sideways to reveal a hidden room. It was about ten meters square and contained enough firepower to start a small uprising.

The Patriot removed a metal flight case from one of the shelves and brought it back out to the control room. As he did, the desk slid back into position by its own volition. He placed the case gently on the desk and flipped the lid.

"Meet Itchy and Scratchy," he said with a flourish. Inside, cocooned in protective foam, were two Israeli built insect-drones—ornithopters. The Patriot gingerly extracted one and held it up to the light, turning it this way and that as he scrutinized it. It looked remarkably like a dragonfly. They were the cutting edge in drone technology. Small, about ten centimeters in length, and semi-autonomous.

"Their wings double as solar arrays, extends their operational time. They can also recharge by landing on any overhead power line." He feathered the fragile wings with his fingers like a vet examining an exotic bird.

"We have a similar pair of these out in the field already," said The Patriot. "Not quite as cool as these little guys, though." He continued examining the drone with an intensity that bordered on obsession. "These guys can have a lethal sting in the tail," he said, placing the drone carefully on the desk.

"This is just a simple reconnaissance mission, Moshe. No killing anyone, okay?" said Mr. Wang.

"Yeah, sure." The Patriot seemed disappointed. "How long do we need to stay on the target?"

"A day or two at most. After that it won't matter."

"Okay, I think we'll use both so that they can rotate. That way we can be operational 24/7 or for as long as is needed. We can also split them up if we see anyone of interest." He extracted the second drone from its foam sarcophagus and then placed them both carefully on the desk.

"I'll need to do a few preliminary checks, all going well we should be good to go in about a half hour." He poked his glasses back up on his nose and sat down to boot up the control systems. "We can get a digital signature of the inspector from the on-board CCTV. That should be good enough for a start. With enough data, they can pick a target out in a crowd and keep a bead on it. Once we get a good visual, we can pretty much let these puppies just follow her around and record what they see."

"Whatever, Moshe. Just keep it low-key for now," said Mr. Wang.

"Sure."

Mr. Wang left him to it. There was no question about it, The Patriot was one scary 21st-century tech-dude. It also struck him that the world just kept inventing evermore creative ways to kill people.

10

CONSIDER IT AN ORDER

Madelaine sucked deep on her Virginia Slim and exhaled a long slow vortex of vapor. She watched it slowly rise and dissipate on the wind as she stood in the open doorway of her office balcony. Overhead, she heard the soft buzzing of a large insect, *zizz, zizz,* then it was gone, lost to the breeze like the smoke.

Her office door opened and Maria poked her head in. "The chief wants a word," she jerked her head in the direction of the commander's office. "Like, now, was the message." She made an apologetic face.

Madelaine nodded and returned her gaze to the harbor, across to the shape of the Helios, its vast bulk nestled alongside the nautical luxury of its palatial neighbors. She took a last pull of her slim and stubbed it out in a battered ashtray fashioned from an old ship's compass. The insect buzzed again as she closed the balcony door and headed off to find the chief.

Very few people in the Monaco Harbor Police actually knew that Régis Onassa, Commander in Chief, was in fact a dear friend of her father. They went back a long way. It was he who put her in line for the job of Detective Inspector and helped her get back on her feet after Mali. He went out on a limb for her and she was thankful, very thankful.

He was sitting in a high-backed leather office chair, facing away from her as she entered. He swung around and smiled. "Ahh...Madelaine, how are you?"

"I'm okay."

"You'll never guess who I was just on the phone to?"

"No, who?"

"Go on, apply some of those finely honed detective skills of yours and have a stab at it."

Madelaine was in no mood for games. Régis Onassa may be a family friend, but he could be sardonic in the extreme when he was of a mind.

"I have no idea."

"Take a wild guess then."

Madelaine sighed. "The Pope?"

"Christ, Madelaine, you never cease to amaze me."

"You were actually taking to the Pope?"

Régis gave a wry smile and wagged a digit in the air. "No, but you're remarkably close. The person I was talking to is also the head of a small European state, none other than our dear leader, Prince Bertrand himself. Imagine that, the Prince taking time out of his busy schedule to give me a call."

"The Lord works in mysterious ways," said Madelaine as she sat down on a low armchair.

"Have a guess what he was talking about."

"Chief, can you cut the crap and get to the point? I have an extremely anxious princess who is concerned that we are not doing everything we can to find her missing Fluffy-Wuffy. The future of the Principality is riding on the outcome."

"Okay, then, the point is...what the hell are you playing at? I mean...what the hell, Madelaine?" He slapped two hands down on the desk and leaned forward.

She feigned ignorance. "Could you be more specific, Chief?"

Régis raised his hand. "Stop, spare me, you know what I'm talking about." He stood up from his chair, hands still resting on the desk. "I had the Prince himself, on the phone, giving me a serious ass kicking. He was wondering what moron was responsible for the search of his best buddy's yacht, and why we were harassing one of the most important patrons of the Principality, and what were we playing at, and who was responsible, and can I have their head on a block, and what the hell...blah, blah, blah. So why don't *you* cut the crap and please enlighten me." He opened both hands out in front of him. "Well?"

Madelaine sighed again. "Well, as Detective Inspector of the Monaco Harbor Police, I have the power to search any boat that takes my fancy, anytime I want. I can even go and stick a microscope up Xiang Zu's ass should I decide to do so. That's what we do here. We're the police."

Régis brought one hand up and rubbed his forehead. He shook his head. "Not the Prince's most treasured patron, not the guy who sponsors the Prince's Trust and a whole bunch of other shit, you do not get to search his yacht, no way, no how. And even if you did stick a microscope up his ass, all you will find is the sun, moon, and stars, because that's what the Prince thinks shines out of it! So, for the love of God, Madelaine, what were you thinking?"

Madelaine slumped back in her chair. She looked down at her hands and thought for a moment. "I got a call this morning, an 817."

"An 817, as in anonymous," said Régis raising an eyebrow.

"Yes, the caller claimed he witnessed a murder aboard Xiang Zu's yacht last night. A young woman, shot through the head at point blank range, her body weighed down and dumped overboard."

The chief sat down at his desk and looked at Madelaine. His tone was quieter. "Do we know where the call came from?"

"We think it came from Nice, from a prepaid number."

He leaned back, the old leather chair squeaking as it took his weight. "Christ, Madelaine, an 817, prepaid phone, that's nothing, you know that. Some cook in the galley gets fired and thinks this would be a bit of a laugh to have the police running all over the place. If we took any of these calls seriously, we would need a force ten times the size. This is crazy, Madelaine."

Madelaine paused. "I know, I know, but there was just

something about it, I can't put my finger on it, just something in the tone."

"Madelaine, you are treading on very dangerous ground here. The Prince wanted your head on a block. His only lament is that the Principality have banned executions in the royal palace since 1847 otherwise you would be up there, tied to a post, your body ventilated with buckshot. You know you can't follow up on this, it's a no-no. For God's sakes Madelaine, someone of your experience, what are you playing at?"

Madelaine looked down and toed the carpet like a schoolgirl brought before the headmistress for stealing sticky buns from the kitchen. "I just...just had to do something, something that resembled police work." She looked up.

"Look, even if you had a video of Xiang Zu repeatedly stabbing a naked girl in a shower to the sound of high-pitched violin strings, you would still never get it to stick. And I don't say that lightly as a Commander in Chief. But these people would destroy you long before their day in court. As it is, you're in deep shit just by searching his yacht. You, of all people, Madelaine, you do not need to put yourself in this jeopardy."

"So are you saying do nothing?"

"Think about it. What have you got? An 817, that's all. You've officially got nothing, nada." He cut the air with his hand. "Yes, technically you can search any boat you want. But all that's going to do for you is make enemies of the wrong people, nothing more." He sat forward in his chair. "Look, I know you're frustrated. I know Monaco is not the sharp end of the crime busting stick, *nothing ever happens in Monaco*, that's what they say, isn't it?"

"They also say *it's a sunny place for shady people*," Madelaine replied, raising an eyebrow.

Régis let out a long sigh. "What I'm saying is...I've got the Prince all over my ass on this one, and he could make life extremely difficult for you. If you push this, then you are going to get your walking papers, and yes...I know it's bullshit, but that's the way it is. So think about what you are doing to yourself. The last thing you need now is to be looking for another job. Think about that. What that would mean for you, all because of an 817?"

"You're right, it's bullshit, this whole place is bullshit." said Madelaine, she folded her arms and sat back in the seat.

"Bullshit or not, I'm on your side on this. The only person I give a crap about is you, so please say you'll drop this."

Madelaine stayed sullen, arms still folded, buried deep in her seat. She looked at the chief. "I'm sorry, don't get me wrong. I appreciate everything you've done for me and Leon, I do, it's just...I don't know...I think I'm just...angry."

Régis let out a stubby laugh. "You know that's actually a good thing, it's a damn sight better than being numb. Means you're putting the past behind. Strange as it may seem, you are getting on with your life. Just don't mess it all up on this. Please tell me you'll drop it."

Madelaine sighed, then nodded. "Okay, to hell with it. You're right, it's stupid."

"Good."

They both relaxed for a moment, Régis leaned back in his office chair. "So, how's Leon doing these days. What is he now, eleven?"

"Twelve. He's doing good, he started playing hockey in school." She thought about the way he had been so withdrawn after his father died. She had kept the manner of his death from him, no child needs to hear that. Yet children are resilient and can bounce back quicker that adults. He had settled well in school with new friends and new activities. She was a fool to jeopardize that. Maybe it was time to stop trying to be a hero and start simply being a mother.

"Why don't you take a bit of time off Madelaine, have a break. Take a week or two, spend some time with Leon."

Madelaine looked up, and began to consider the proposal. "You know something, Chief, I just might do that. In fact, it sounds like a good idea. All the security arrangements for the Fusion Conference are in place, and there's not much else on that Maria can't cover. So, I suppose I could take some time." She locked eyes with the chief. "How would tomorrow sound?"

Régis was slightly taken aback by the speed of Madelaine's response. "Eh... sure, why not? It will be good for you." He paused for a moment then leaned forward across the desk. "Actually, there's something you can do for me before you go, consider it your last duty before the break."

"That depends. What is it?"

"The Art Exhibition, this evening, another one of the Prince's pet projects. Anyway, it's a state event and the police need to be represented. I'd go but I'm... eh... not able to, so I want you to go in my place."

Madelaine thought about this. "Is there nobody else? You know I'm not good at these sorts of public things, I just feel like a spare part."

"What's there to be good at? Just show up, look at some art, and drink some champagne. It's pretty simple really. Anyway, Maria's going, her boyfriend has a few paintings at it, so you can go together and represent the Department."

"I'm not sure, I'll need to check on babysitting."

Régis gave a big smile. "Consider it an order. Remember you owe me one. I'll give Maria the details, she can get it organized for you. Hey, Madelaine, you might actually enjoy it." He gave an expansive gesture with his hands.

Madelaine sighed. "Why do I get the feeling I'm being set up?"

11

THE DUDE ABIDES

Charles Gardner dozed on the stern deck of the Ave Maria, the Bimini top canopy shading him from the intense afternoon sun. A gentle breeze feathered his face, and on the table beside him balanced the remains of two fingers of Irish whiskey. His semi-intoxicated body lay dormant across the bench, yet his senses accepted the sounds of the marina, the other sounds, the ones less heard: the slap of a halyard on metal masts like the peal of church bells, the cry of gulls as they swooped and circled, the lap of water against the hull. All these sounds came into his subconscious like a hypnotic hymn and time ceased to have meaning. He was neither awake nor asleep, neither conscious nor unconscious and it was at these times that Jenny would come and talk to him.

"I wonder who she was?" Her voice was a whisper.

"Who?"

"The woman with the bullet through her head."

He had a sense of Jenny sitting across from him, relaxing against the bulkhead, a pink straw sun hat shading her face.

"Whoever she was, she's gone now."

"Are you going to save her, Charlie?"

"I can't save her, Jenny. She's dead, she sleeps with the fishes."

"Dead, like me."

"Don't say that."

"Wait... I hear Leonie." Her voice drifted away on the breeze.

Far off amongst the myriad of marina chatter a car door closed and a voice spoke, he recognized it, the familiar tone embedded in his parental DNA. It brought him back to the light.

Charles rose from the bench and scanned the marina. Up at the head of the walkway stood Leonie, a taxi leaving behind her as she held her hand over her eyes and peered in his direction. He stood up, clambered over the stern railing onto the walkway and waved. By the third wave she spotted him and waved back, jumping in the air as she did. She gathered a bag and her two companions, ran down the walkway, and threw a big hug around him.

"Daaaaad."

Charles laughed.

She stood back and gripped his arms in both hands and

looked at him. "Dad, oh my god, you look so skinny, you haven't been eating, what have you been living on?"

"Oh... I decided a while back to see if I could just live off only the fish I could catch."

"What!"

"Just joking," he laughed.

By now her two companions had caught up. She turned and gestured at them with an expansive arm. "This is David and Kats, the rest of the team. David's our cameraman and Kats does the research and keeps me on the straight and narrow."

David extended a hand. "Mr. Gardner, good to finally meet you." Charles felt a reassured grip. He shook it and then extended a hand to Kats. A preemptive move on his part, just in case she had any plan to kiss him on both cheeks, as is the French way in these here parts.

"Mr. Gardner." She nodded as she shook his hand.

"Call me Charles. Come," he said as he turned, one arm still around Leonie's shoulders. "Welcome to my humble abode."

They clambered on board, Charles helping Kats with her balance as she stepped onto the Ave Maria. "So, Leonie, here you finally are." It was Charles's turn to hold her by the shoulders and appraise her. "You've just been a blur of emails and messages these last few months."

"Yes, I know. It's been very busy, Dad. Gotta pay the rent, you know. We all can't go swanning around the Med for a living."

"So, you're the new face of the channel."

"Ha, just one of a lot of faces, Dad. Nothing special."

Charles glanced over at her companions, who were looking unsure of what to do.

"Why don't you both head down to the galley and grab us a couple of cold ones from the fridge. Glasses are just above in the cupboard, if you have a desire to be civilized. I'll have mine by the neck."

"Sure thing." David nodded, and they descended the companionway, disappearing below.

"Hope you don't mind me bringing the production crew," said Leonie, a little apologetically. "They were dying to see the boat. I think they thought it was one of the super yachts and you were some kind of mega-rich dude."

"No problem, and sorry to disappoint. So tell me, what's the channel got planned for you in Monaco?"

"We have a truck load interviews lined up for tomorrow, plus a full report on the significance of fusion power, and then of course there's the big event itself—the ignition test. It's the science gig of the century."

Kats returned with an arm full of beers. David trailed after with glasses. They popped the beers and sat down. Charles raised his bottle and said, "So what shall we drink to?"

"How about health, wealth, and happiness in your preferred order?" offered David.

Charles laughed, "Sounds good to me." They raised their drinks and clinked. "So are you guys all set for the big event? The launch of ITER, the future of cheap clean energy, and the salvation of human civilization as we know it?"

"If it doesn't blow up," said Kats. "Remember what happened at Livermore last year?"

"Yes," said Charles. "That was a tragedy. Something went very wrong with the test."

"Sure did," Kats responded. "Livermore was first up to the mark with a sustainable fusion reactor. The test firing was a major media event. Just one slight problem, the place blew up killing five people and injuring a load of others."

"But ITER is a completely different system." David waved his beer around and shook his head. "Livermore was using lasers and their setup wasn't properly designed for sustainable fusion. They were pushing their luck. ITER, on the other hand, has been engineered from the ground up for this singular purpose. It's not going to go boom."

"Rumor has it that what happened at Livermore was sabotage." Kats responded, her voice low and conspiratorial.

"That's just paranoia, the internet rumor mill. There's no evidence for that. The reason it blew up is simply because the containment system failed," said David.

"Yes, but why did *that* fail?" countered Kats.

"Well, it seems to me," said Charles, "that part of the reason the ITER launch is such a big media event is the ghoulish anticipation that it will, in fact, blow up."

Leonie laughed. "Ha, some things never change, do they? Anyway, we can talk about it later, okay?" She gave a look to her crew who both nodded in unison. "We have lots to do before then, which brings me to my present." She opened her bag and fished out a gilt-edged envelope with the Royal Monaco seal emblazoned on the top corner. "I've got you an invite to the Royal Monaco Art Exhibition this evening."

"Wow, really? The Cote d'Azur exhibition, how did you manage that? They're, like, gold dust." Charles opened the envelope and slid out the ornate invite, examining it with a sense of deference and awe.

"We're doing a piece on it for the channel, so I managed to blag an official ticket for you," said Leonie.

"What can I say? Thanks, this is great. I tried to get one before I came, but I would need to be related to the Prince to get in." He held the invite in both hands, not quite convinced that he was really holding an official ticket. "You know, this year they'll have all the masters as well as the contemporary guys and a whole bunch of the new kids on the block."

"Just one thing dad. You can't go dressed like that. Do you have you something decent to wear?" Leonie gave him the one over.

Charles looked down at his attire. "What's wrong with this?" he looked over at David for backup.

"No way, Dad, you can't show up to the poshest art exhibition this side of Buckingham Palace in shorts and a t-shirt. Especially one with a picture of Jeff Bridges and a slogan that says *The dude abides*, no way." She stood up. "Come on, let's see what you've got down below." She headed down the companionway.

Charles stood up to follow. He turned to Leonie's friends and shrugged his shoulders. "Better follow orders."

Dave laughed and raised his beer. "For what it's worth, I think that t-shirt's a work of art."

Leonie was already in the main cabin staring in to her dad's meagre wardrobe. "Seriously dad, don't you have anything other than shorts and t-shirts?"

"Hey, it's the Med, I live on a boat. What more do I need?"

"Well, we'll need to get you something."

"Hold on," said Charles. He moved over to the bunk and with one hand lifted the bottom section. It hinged itself up with the help of some gas springs to reveal a big storage area. He reached in and lifted out a large case. "I keep the good linen in here. Haven't had a reason to wear any of it before now. Might need an iron though." He unzipped the case at one end to expose a hanger. He then lifted the case up and hung it on the cabin wall as he unzipped the rest. As he did, it unfolded itself until, finally, he undid the airtight seal down the center. Inside he had two suits and a few shirts. He looked over at Leonie. "See what you think, I have some more here." He pulled another case from the bed storage and proceeded to unpack it. After twenty minutes, he had three of these cases unpacked. "Airtight clothes storage," he proudly announced. "I've also rigged a dehumidifier in this cabin directed through the storage space. Clever eh?"

"Okay, Dad, I stand amazed as usual."

"Ah...it's old school really."

She looked into the bed storage area. "What's in that one?"

"Oh, eh...that's nothing, just some other stuff."

"Well come on, let's have a look."

"Well...it's...eh...actually it's some of your mother's clothes."

Leonie was silenced. She looked at her dad.

"I know...I know...what's the point and all that, it's just... some things are hard to let go of."

Leonie put her hand on his shoulder. "I know, Dad, it's okay, but you do need to move on at some point."

"Yeah...I know, but if you spend twenty years with someone it's just not that easy."

Leonie stared at the suitcase for a moment. "I miss her too, Dad, we all do. You know sometimes I think that I might be forgetting her face." She looked up at her dad. "I have to take out her photograph just to remind myself."

Charles closed the bed and sat down on the end, his arms on his knees, his hands clasped. He stared at the floor. "Maybe I've been away too long, Leonie. Trying to escape, to run away. Perhaps I need to head home."

Leonie sat down beside him. "We worry about you, Dad. Worry that you're all right."

"I know. I'm just a stupid old man, full of grief and ghosts. I need to come back to the light." He smiled at Leonie. "I'm glad you're here. I've been really looking forward to it, you know."

"Me too," said Leonie.

Charles rubbed his face and slapped his knees. "I'm fine, really I am. Let's get back up to your friends, back to the living, eh?" He smiled again.

She gave him a hug. "Sure. Back to the living it is."

They headed out of the main cabin and through the saloon.

"I'll just grab a few more beers," said Charles, as he looked into the cooler, assessing the provisions. Up top, he could overhear the conversation going on between David and Kats.

"It's not going to blow up." David sounded emphatic.

"It could." Kats was still not convinced.

"That's just being paranoid."

"Well, as Andrew S. Grove, ex-CEO of Intel, once said, 'Only the paranoid survive,'" replied Kats with a hint of triumph.

"I heard he ended up in an asylum suffering from paranoid schizophrenia." David was not giving up.

"Really? Is that true?"

"No, just kidding."

"Very funny. Ha, bloody ha."

Leonie came up from the salon.

"Did you find some suitable attire for your dad?" asked Kats.

"Yes, he seems to have engineered a state-of-the-art clothes storage systems for yachts, from which he magicked a few Armani suits, no less."

"Cool," said David. "The dude abides."

"Simple engineering, really," said Charles as he emerged from the salon and began passing around more beers. "The curse of all boating activity is the damp," he said as he sat down again. "It gets into everything. Fortunately, here in the Med, the problem is minimal. However, it's not completely eliminated. The worst thing is having a damp place to sleep, so I rigged up a small dehumidifier and routed it through the base of my bed so it keeps me dry and anything that I need to have dry storage for."

"What do you do for power?" Dave glanced around the deck.

"Two wind turbines on the stern and most of the Bimini top is covered in solar panels." He jabbed a finger up at the canopy. "I generate more than enough to power everything on the boat."

"So what do you think of the ITER project, Mr. Gardner?" Kats asked.

"Charles, call me Charles. A sure sign of getting old is when adults start calling you mister, and I'm not that old just yet." He gave a laugh. "I'll tell you what I think of ITER, but first you must all stay for a spot of lunch." He looked over at Leonie for confirmation.

She seemed a bit flustered. This was not part of her carefully orchestrated plan. "Well, eh... I'm not sure if we have time. We still have a few interviews to line up and equipment to check, and—"

"Well, you can do all that from here. Anyway I've been on the water for months and could do with some company. So what do you say?" He opened his hands in an inviting gesture.

"I've got a few calls to make, but are you sure you don't mind if I make them here?" asked Kats.

"Of course not." Charles slapped his knees. "That's settled then. You're all staying for lunch."

12

CLEAN SHAVED AND SOBER

David slowly stirred the pasta sauce with a wooden spoon and couldn't resist tasting it. "Mmmmm... this is great, Charles. What's in it?"

Charles was busy gathering up plates and cutlery and laying out the small dining table on board the Ave Maria. "Oh, this and that, mushrooms, white wine, garlic, parmesan, and a few other bits and bobs."

"Well, it's yummy."

"Just keep stirring it, make sure the heat is low."

"Aye, aye, Captain."

Kats had ensconced herself at the navigation station and was busy making calls. From the little that Charles had heard, it seemed mainly about the Art Exhibition this evening rather than the Fusion Conference. Leonie had spent most of the time up on deck enjoying the sun, working on her tan. Charles stuck his head out the salon hatch. "Chow's ready."

"Oh, great, I'm starving. I haven't eaten properly since we left London."

They all gathered around the small table while Charles dug out a bottle of wine from the cooler. He handed it to David with a corkscrew. "Would you do the honors?"

"A pleasure."

Charles then busied himself with getting the food out onto the table. Pasta, baked chicken with oregano, mushroom sauce, and some garlic bread.

"Wow, this smells great. I'm so hungry." David popped the cork from the wine bottle and poured out some glasses.

"Ah, it's just a quick throw together," said Charles as he put the last of the dishes on the table and sat down. The others were obviously hungry and busied themselves getting food onto their plates with a general chorus of mmmm... and such like. Charles grabbed his wine glass and raised it. "To health, wealth, and happiness in your preferred order." They clinked together and laughed.

Charles was happy, the happiest he'd been in a long time. Sitting here with Leonie and her friends, he felt content. They all ate and drank with the enthusiasm of the very hungry. After a while, they settled down and the conversation turned to the main event—fusion. It was Kats who spoke first.

"So what do you think of this whole ITER fusion thing, Charles?"

"Well, I don't think ITER have come this far just to fail. Worst case scenario is they don't get as much out as they had hoped for, but it's just the first of many tests. So yeah, I think they'll succeed—and probably change the world as we know it."

"Really?" David raised an eyebrow at Charles as he guided another forkful of pasta into his mouth. "You don't think it's just a ridiculously expensive experiment that isn't actually going to make much of a difference?"

Charles shook his head. "No. I think it will be nothing short of momentous. You see, you need to think about it in terms of global clean energy demand." Charles rose from the table and headed over to the galley to make some coffee for everyone. "Let's imagine for a moment, David, that you're the leader of a developing country."

"Can I be the King?"

Charles glanced over at him and smiled. "Sure."

"Cool, it's good to be the King." David then adopted an imperial air and held the back of his hand out to Kats. "You may kiss the royal ring."

"Go kiss my ass." She elbowed him.

"Later, darling, later." He winked.

Kats rolled her eyes to heaven. "You should come with a warning label."

"Anyway," Charles continued. "Your subjects need more energy because the economy is booming and they now want to populate their homes with a raft of new appliances. Since you're a good king, you need to build a new power station, so here are your choices. Oil and gas are a possibility, but they spew out greenhouse gasses and damage the environment—not ideal. Also, the country you get it from may not like you anymore and stop selling it to you, wrecking your economy."

"What about renewables?" asked the King.

"Sure, but you would need an awful lot of windfarms and solar panels, not to mention energy storage, to get anywhere near the stability of oil or gas. The industrialists might get angry with you if they don't have enough power for their factories when the wind doesn't blow and the sun don't shine— and then your economy starts to suffer."

"Nuclear, then?"

"Yeah, but it's a massive capital investment, politically fraught, and if something went wrong, large swathes your country could be turned into a wasteland." Charles sat down with a pot of coffee and some small espresso cups. "You see, in the end you'll probably just go for coal, because it's cheap and available—and screw the planet."

"I'm a bad King." David stuck his bottom lip put and hung his head. They all laughed.

"There are still hundreds of coal power plants being built all over the globe." Leonie threw her two cents into the conversation. "For developing countries, it's the option of choice and it's the worst for the planet."

"So fusion is the answer to the world's energy problems then," said Kats.

"It's *an* answer," said Charles. "It's clean and virtually limitless." He poured the coffee. "The only thing is, nobody's got it to work yet."

"ITER has cost over twenty billion and counting." Kats sipped her coffee. "That's a crazy amount of money to spend on a science experiment."

"Is it?" Charles replied. "Sure, it's a lot of cash, but think of what the International Space Station cost? It's topped a hundred and fifty billion. NASA's SLS rocket cost over fifty billion. Or what about all the money spent on, say, election campaigning? Or the trillions spent on war for that matter. Would you say that was good value for money?" Charles shook his head. "The world is full of waste—money spent on the self-aggrandizement of nation states or egotistical pursuit of special interests." He gave a long slow sigh. He was beginning to lecture, something Jenny would pick him up on when he started to get carried away in company. "All I'm saying is that, if it works, then it will probably be the best twenty billion we ever spent."

"I'll drink to that." David raised his glass. They all clinked.

"But there's more to the development of fusion power than just ITER." It was Leonie's turn to take up the baton. "The Chinese are on the moon mining helium3 for their own fusion reactors, and the word from the science community is that they will be ready later this year."

"You gotta hand it to them," said David "The US went up there and all they did was plant flags and drive around in their SUVs. The Chinese don't mess around, it's straight down to business—extract the resources."

"The thing is," Leonie continued, "is that a helium3 fusion reactor is *theoretically* way more efficient than the reactor design at ITER. So, if they do succeed, then we're into a technology war. That's why it's so important for ITER to have a successful ignition test tomorrow. Otherwise the Chinese could steal a march on them and make it all technically redundant."

"Well, that's the techno-politics of it. Way too complicated for my simple mind to fathom," said Charles, who was now rummaging around in some locker in the galley. He pulled out a bottle of twenty-five-year-old Irish whiskey and examined it. "I've been saving this for a special occasion, now seems like as good an occasion as any."

"Oh... now you're talking," said David.

"Hey, David, remember you've got a job to do later, like holding a camera steady," said a stern-faced Kats.

David feigned umbrage. "Never come between a man and his whiskey. It's like removing a limb—a very important limb."

Charles poured four small glasses and handed one to each. "To your good health and a steady hand, sir," he said, and he raised his drink.

David plopped an ice cube in his drink and sniffed the pungent liquor with the air of a connoisseur, then he sipped it like it was nectar of the gods. "This is a damn fine whiskey, Captain."

"Just don't get wasted," warned Kats.

David looked across at Charles. "Don't get me wrong, I love the work, it's just the people can be so cruel, you know." He hung his head down in mock abjection and shook it.

Charles laughed. "So how come you guys are not covering

the main event over in ITER? How come you're here at the Fusion Conference, surely that's the side show?"

"We're the B team," said Leonie, who was just taking her first sip of the whiskey. "Whoa... that's got a kick to it." Her face scrunched up like a beer can in a crusher.

"There's a few select media channels invited to the main event. Apparently there's not much room, or so they say," said Kats.

"We're not worthy," said David. "Anyway, we're to cover the Art Expo this evening first, then it's the Fusion Conference here in Monaco tomorrow. Unless of course the A team chickened out, and we're needed to save the day."

"Why would they chicken out?" Charles asked in between sips.

"Ha, because they're pompous prima donnas who are afraid their hair might get ruined if the place blew up." David ran a hand through his curly locks.

"It's a possibility," said Kats.

"Don't be daft." David replied with a roll of his eyes.

"They haven't shown up yet," said Kats. It was a comment meant for her colleagues, she said it like it was a kind of premonition.

Leonie exchanged a look with her in a serious, raised eyebrow kind of way, but said nothing. She then glanced at her watch. "I think it's time we went and got ourselves ready." She stood up from the table. The others all moved themselves into the vertical and started gathering their bits. Hugs and air kisses were exchanged as they made their way out of the salon on to the deck of the Ave Maria.

"So you'll stay here tonight?" said Charles. It was directed at Leonie.

She kissed him on the cheek and gave him a hug. "Of course. Kats and David are staying at the hotel." She looked over at them as they made their way along the boardwalk. She was just about to step off the boat. "I'll see you later at the exhibition. But remember, I'll be working."

"Sure, no problem. I'll keep a low profile." He gave her a smile.

"And don't come in a t-shirt," she called back as she stepped off the boat.

"Ha, don't worry, I'll be clean shaved and sober."

13

A STOLEN MOMENT

By the time Marcel returned to Monaco, it was that part of the day when afternoon activities had wound down but evening had not yet begun. As the sun began to set, Marcel parked the motorbike below the main harbor promenade, close to the Helios. He didn't want to bring it back on board just yet, he wasn't in the mood for talking to Nikolai. The big Russian mechanic was probably still pissed off with him for slamming his head into the stern bay door.

His body was stiff from the long ride and just a little cold. He stretched as he got off, nurtured some feeling back into his muscles, and started up the gangplank at the stern of the Helios.

"Hey, Marcel!" It was one of the new security personnel. There had been so many new people of late, Marcel had difficulty keeping track, he thought the guy's name might be *Park*.

"Mr. Wang wants you to report to him as soon as you're on board. He's up in the operations room." He jerked a thumb at the upper deck.

"Okay." Marcel nodded and moved toward the steps. He glanced back as he ascended and could see Park talking into his cuff and signaling to two others. They looked up at Marcel and started to follow. He didn't recognize them. *New guys,* he thought, and kept going.

A few minutes later, Marcel entered the operations room, the nerve center of the ship. On the giant main screen, a desolate lunar landscape stretched off into the distance while, in the foreground, lunar rovers moved to and fro, earning their keep in the Xiang Zu empire.

The operations room had a full complement of people this evening. On the lower level, several technicians were illuminated by glow of data screens. On the upper level, Xiang Zu sat with Mr. Wang and Lao Bang. Xiang's pet chameleon was perched on the desk in front of him, rotating an imperious eye in Marcel's direction.

"Ah, Marcel, I see you're impressed with our lunar endeavors. Good of you to join us, I trust the mission was successful?" Xiang Zu was seated as always behind his elaborate antique desk. The chameleon started to rock back and forth.

"Yes, no problems. He's planning to have the device in place this evening," said Marcel as he entered the upper level.

"Excellent, excellent. Do take a seat. There's something Mr. Wang wants to show you."

As Marcel went to sit down, he noticed the two new security guys enter the room and take up standing positions behind him, one either side. He got a feeling that something was going down. Marcel unbuttoned his jacket and sat forward in the chair. That way he could reach the knife he kept strapped to the base of his spine—just in case.

"Mr. Wang, if you would be so kind as to show Marcel the video." Xiang Zu waved at his head of security. Mr. Wang's hand danced over a tablet computer and a dark and grainy video materialized on screen. It was Marika's cabin, night-time, two people in the throes of passion—Marika and Marcel.

"What the hell is this?" Marcel exclaimed.

Mr. Wang tapped the tablet again and the image froze on screen where both could clearly be seen. "It would appear that you've been sleeping with the enemy."

"Hey, a man's got to do what a man's got to do," Marcel shrugged, trying to act casual. "You know how it is."

"But how do we know you weren't in bed with her in more ways than one?" Xiang Zu looked Marcel over the top of his glasses.

Marcel stiffened. "What are you saying?"

"It's a question of trust, Marcel," Xiang Zu replied.

"So I get hot with some woman and that makes me a spy?" Marcel jumped up from his seat. As he did, the two security guys pounced on him. He tried to twist around and reach for his knife, but a Beretta M9 dug into his ribs.

"Face down on the table." The security guy said as the gun moved up to the back of Marcel's head, pushing him down. They frisked him, removing his pistol, knife, and Marika's diary.

"What's this?" The security guy threw the diary over to Mr. Wang, who examined it and then passed it over to Xiang Zu.

"It's just her diary. I couldn't throw it away," said Marcel.

"You were supposed to get rid of everything, every last scrap of her existence," said Mr. Wang.

Xiang Zu stood up and walked over to Marcel. "I am disappointed in you. But more than that, I'm disappointed in myself. I feel that I failed you in some way, that my teachings were lacking in some respect. That I did not try hard enough to eradicate the street dog in you." He waved his hands expansively in the air. "But if it's any consolation to you, I have learned a great lesson here today—that I too have my moments of fallibility." He turned abruptly and sat back down. "Take him down below and lock him up. We'll deal with him later."

"This is crazy, I'm no goddamn spy." But Marcel knew there was no use in trying to fight his way out. He'd get a bullet in the head, just like Marika. They hauled him up and marched him to the door. He turned and took one last look at the frozen images on the screen. A stolen moment, a moment of happiness, gone forever.

14

GALLERY

The Royal Annual Monaco Art Expo is a gathering of pure splendor, started in 1956 by an influential cohort of French and American art dealers who saw the influx of vacationing wealth to the region as an opportunity not to be missed. As Hollywood money descended on the fabled Mediterranean enclave, the purveyors of the *must have* wall accessory for your cozy villa were sure to follow. Royal patronage ensued in the 1960s, and, in the 1980s, it morphed into one of the most important annual events for the tiny Principality. By the early 21st century, it had become one of the world's major art shows. Part exhibition, part works for sale, showcasing both established dealers and up and coming stars of the art world. It was also the absolute *must be seen at* gathering for the aristocracy and the filthy rich.

Charles Gardner, however, was neither of these.

Nevertheless, he was a lifelong aficionado of all things painterly and was giddy as a child at the prospect of going to the opening night. He fingered the invite in the pocket of his recently excavated Armani suit as he walked up to the entrance. *This is going to be great,* he thought.

Inside the exhibition's main hall, Leonie, Kats, and David were not so giddy. They were deep in discussions on how best to get what they needed to produce a half hour of reportage. Most of their prep work had been done around the Fusion Conference, so the Art Expo was somewhat of an afterthought. However, by way of getting more bang for their buck, the channel had been required by the principality to cover the event, notwithstanding the fact that Monaco was a significant advertiser.

"We can get a few sweeping shots of the glitterati, maybe up there from the balcony?" said Leonie. David nodded.

"Then some close ups of the art. We can overdub with reportage, you know, the salient points. Okay?" David and Kats both nodded.

"Then we need to do the interviews. So, who have we got?"

Kats consulted her lists. "Penciled in is the Prince himself, we've got about a minute, then we've got some state officials, chamber of commerce, Harbor Police, et cetera." She looked up from the list.

"Well, we're going to need more than that, have you got anything else lined up? I mean, we have every aristocrat on the planet here with two cents to rub together, we must be able to do better than the Harbor Police," said Leonie.

Kats consulted her list again, flicking through pages and getting flustered.

"Why don't you prioritize by rank?" offered David. "You know, start with kings, then queens, and work your way down."

"Hey, this isn't a deck of cards," Kats replied with a twinge of frustration.

"Any aces in there?" David leaned over to look at the list.

"Ha-ha, very funny," said Kats.

He stabbed a finger at a name on the list, "Well, I'll be damned, there's an ace."

"There is?" Kats looked at the list.

"Farah Pahlavi, the Empress of Iran—that has to top the list, that's an ace."

"No, it's not."

"Yes, it is. Empress is one up from a mere King, gotta be," said David.

"How can there be an Empress of Iran? It's a theocracy," Kats replied, clearly confused.

"Damned if I know, maybe it's an *artist formally known as...* kind of thing." David was now scanning the list with even more interest.

"Look here," he stabbed the list again. "There's a Princess Bacardi. I wonder if she comes with coke."

"You're hilarious." Kats rolled her eyes.

"Will you guys just cut it out, this is not helping," said Leonie. "David, start getting some shots. Kats, get working that list and get some face time organized. I'll go and track down some of the commoners." David and Kats nodded, a little sheepish.

"We could also do with interviewing someone who actually knows something about art, but I may just have the man for that. All right then, let's get to work."

"Blackbush, two ice cubes."

"Certainly, sir."

Charles scanned the vast array of hard liquor that was ever so artistically displayed along the back wall of the gallery bar and was pleased to see a decent selection of Irish whiskey. While the barman went about the business at hand, Charles flicked through a voluminous tome festooned with princely insignia, which was the exhibition catalog. After a quick scan, his biggest fear had abated, and that was the prospect of an exhibition filled with *installations*. He took a sip of his drink and felt the warmth rise in his throat. *Irish whiskey, no installations, the omens are looking good,* he thought.

There was a time when a painting could animate an entire society. From the earliest cave paintings, seen for the first time by simple stone age people, right up to the last century and the shock of the new from the likes of Warhol and Lichtenstein, some paintings had the power to reset one's perspective on the society in which we live, but those days were long gone. In a world swarming with imagery, the craft of painting had long lost its ability to evoke awe, and so *the installation* was born. From the gigantic twenty-six-meter-tall yellow bath duck in Kowloon harbor by Florentijn Hofman to Christo and Jeanne-Claude, who wrapped an entire section of the coast of Little Bay in Sydney in plastic, the installation had become the leading edge of art. However, Charles was a traditionalist, to him it was *total crap*, second only to performance art, which was *complete crap*. He took another sip and headed off into the depths of the exhibition.

Woman with Pink Sun Hat–Oil on Canvas. Charles stared at the painting. If he had a goatee, now would be the time he'd be stroking it. The woman—her back turned to the viewer—faced out over a clear blue Mediterranean Sea. In the distance, a luxury yacht was in full sail. She cradled a small, long-haired dog. Its little head peeked over her right shoulder, directly at the viewer. Its eyes forlorn, almost pleading.

Charles shook his head and turned away from the painting with a sigh. It was then he recognized the inspector who had searched his boat earlier. She was a few meters away, staring intently at an abstract painting. Her back was to him, yet he was certain it was Inspector Madelaine Duchamp. He walked over, stood beside her, and looked at the painting. It consisted of wavy horizontal bands of soft colors.

"No people," he said after a moment.

She glanced around at him. "Pardon?"

"The painting. It has no people in it." He pointed.

"Ahhh, mister... eh?" A note of recognition.

"Gardner."

"Ah, yes. We visited your boat today."

"Indeed." He looked back at the painting. "It's a landscape, you know."

"A landscape?"

"Yes, see?" Charles waved his arm around.

Madelaine looked bemused. "Well, you got me on that one. To my eyes it looks like wavy bands of soft colors. How is that a landscape?"

"Let me show you, stand back a bit, you're too close." They took a few steps back.

"See, the bottom is dark reds and browns, earthy colors. Above that are greens, fields and foliage. Then darker bands of purple for distant mountains, leading to the softer blues and whites of the sky."

Madelaine studied the painting. "You know, you're right. I didn't see it that way."

"I thought that would be an essential skill for an Inspector, looking at things from a different angle?"

"People! Mr. Gardner, not things. The skill is looking at the situations people get themselves into."

"Ahhh, back to people. You know, you had me trying to paint people all afternoon."

She smiled. "Sorry about that. How did you get on?"

Charles thought for a moment. "Not very well. I ended up down at the main harbor, painting a boat called the Helios." He turned to her. "You know it?"

The question hung.

"Everyone in Monaco knows the Helios and Xiang Zu," she finally answered.

Charles fumbled around in his jacket pocket and fished out the card she had given him on the boat that morning. He looked at it. "You know, I did see something *unusual* last night."

"Well, you should report to the Harbor Office first thing in the morning, Mr. Gardner." She turned to go.

"Maybe I'll phone it in instead," he said. "That way it can be anonymous, from a Mr. Smith perhaps."

Madelaine turned back, her face betraying the sudden realization that here was the source of the call.

"Dad!"

Crap! thought Charles as he turned to see Leonie striding toward him with purpose. David was right behind wrestling with a camera.

"Dad, just the man for the job." Then she saw Madelaine and paused.

"Eh... Leonie, this is Inspector Madelaine Duchamp of the Monaco Harbor Police." He turned to Madelaine. "My daughter, Leonie."

"Ah yes, the science journalist," said Madelaine nodding. "We've met. I had to do an interview earlier."

"Thank you for that," said Leonie. "Speaking of which, Dad. I need an interview with someone who actually knows something about art."

"No way." Charles stepped back his hands waving. "No way."

Then Kats showed up with a clipboard in hand. Charles considered that there were probably whole armies of people with clipboards who ran most of the world. They were the people who made sure things got done, the trains ran, the post got delivered and, more importantly, the interviews happened.

"Kats, we need five minutes here with my dad, he's an art expert, believe it or not."

Kats consulted her clipboard, whisked a pen out from nowhere and, with all the glee of a cleric stabbing a vampire through the heart, ticked another one off the list. "Perfect!"

"Wait a minute, are you serious Leonie?" said Charles. "I mean, what am I going to say?"

Leonie was now standing beside her dad, the channel microphone in hand as David hoisted the camera on his shoulder. "You'll be wicked," said David as a blinding light flicked on.

"Right, Dad, look at me, don't look at the camera, I'll do that." Before he knew it, she had started. "We're here with Mr. Charles Gardner, an art expert and regular attendee at the Monaco Art Expo," she turned to Charles. "So, Mr. Gardner what do you think of the exhibition this year?" She thrust the microphone at him, his cue to say something deep and meaningful.

"Er... well, yes... the show has always had a certain... *je nes se quoi*... and this year is... eh... no exception." He paused, then to his own surprise, he got going. "In fact, I noted a dearth of installations in this year's show. It would seem there is a return to the more fundamental disciplines of painting and sculpture. Perhaps this is a reflection of the values of our time."

"Indeed, and have you any favorites at this year's show?"

"Well, interestingly enough, I am particularly taken by this painting right here." They moved so the painting could be in shot, on either side. "At first glance, it looks like wavy horizontal bands of soft colors. But what the artist has cleverly done is chart the journey of the damned from the soft blues of the ethereal soul as it breaks through the bands of birth, journeying down through the green pastures of life and ultimately into darkness and the demonic eternity that is the fiery abyss below."

"Ohh—kay, well thank you, Mr. Gardner, for that fascinating insight into some of the contemporary art at this year's show." She turned to the camera. "This is Leonie Gardner, reporting from the Royal Monaco Art Expo." She smiled. David flicked the light off, and lowered the camera.

"I knew you'd be wicked," said David.

Charles looked over to see that Madelaine had remained, waiting for the interview to finish.

"Leonie, we've got Princess Saliva and the Duchess of Bree lined up in ten at the main reception," announced Kats as she flicked a page on her clipboard.

"Excellent," said Leonie. "Gotta go, Dad, that was great. Catch you later." And they headed off.

"I thought it was a landscape?" said Madelaine.

"As I said, depends what perspective you're looking at it from."

"'The damned,' really?" Her eyebrows raised.

Charles looked down and scratched his chin. "Perhaps I was talking about myself. I'm damned if I do and damned if I don't."

They were silent for a beat as Charles took stock of their surroundings. He then pointed in the direction of a large veranda opening out over the harbor.

"Why don't we head out there, where it's quieter, and we can talk about it."

Madelaine considered this proposal for a second or two as she looked over in the direction of the veranda. It was quiet. Most of the people were inside, downstairs in the main gallery.

"Okay. But are you sure you want to do this?" She turned back and gave him a studied look.

Charles shrugged his shoulders. "I feel I owe it to myself."

They walked out onto the veranda. Charles grabbed two glasses of champagne from a passing waiter. If he was going to put himself on the line with the inspector, he needed a drink. Something stronger than champagne would be preferable, but, under the circumstances, it would have to do.

It was a spacious outside area lit by lanterns, with tables dotted here and there. They headed over to where there were few people and sat at a table overlooking the main Monte Carlo harbor. In the distance, the brooding shape of the Helios was silhouetted by a full moon. It was Madelaine who spoke first. "So, Mr. Gardner, or should I call you Mr. Smith?"

"That would depend on whether you're on or off duty, I suppose."

"As of my interview with your daughter for the channel, I'm officially off for a few weeks."

"Then call me Charles." He took a sip of his drink and looked out over the harbor at shape of the Helios. "Do you think he'll get away with it?"

Madelaine lit a cigarette. She took a long drag and sat back in her chair. "There's nothing to get away with. Apart from some crank call, officially nothing has happened."

"Would anything happen if it was official?"

Madelaine took another drag on her cigarette and considered Charles. "Something would happen all right, but it wouldn't be what you expect, nor very pleasant." She leaned across the table and in almost a whisper she said. "You really have no idea what you are dealing with here." She looked over at the silhouette of the Helios.

"So tell me, what am I dealing with?"

Madelaine flicked the ash from her cigarette and sat back in her chair for a moment, not saying anything. Finally, she leaned across the table again, this time she was being deadly serious. "You need to get out of here, Mr. Gardner, as soon as possible."

"Get out?" Charles was surprised. "I've only just got here, and I'm enjoying it, and call me Charles."

"This is no joke! These are very powerful and dangerous people you are playing with. Listen to me"—she looked around and then back at Charles—"they're looking for you."

Charles was shaken. "How do you know that?" His voice was low, gone was the bravado.

"We just do. One of Xiang Zu's people was snooping around looking for a list of sailing yachts that came in last night."

Charles considered this for a moment. "So, you believe the story, then?"

Madelaine sighed and flicked ash from her cigarette. "I don't have to believe it. If it's true, then your life is in danger. If not, then they are looking for someone else."

Charles took another sip and sat back in his chair. The night air was warm and he felt a trickle of sweat run down the inside of his arm. Overhead he heard the soft buzz of a large insect going about its nocturnal business, *zizz... zizz.* He looked up. "You know, you've got some big insects in this town."

Madelaine looked up, scanning the night sky for source of the sound, but made no comment.

"Would it make a difference if I had it all on video?" He glanced over to see her reaction.

Madelaine eyes widened. "Video?"

"My binoculars have night vision, and a record function. It stored what I saw on an SD card. Do you want it?"

Madelaine lit up another cigarette and said nothing for a while. Finally, she leaned in again. "I shouldn't be telling you this, but, since I'm officially off duty, I'm going to anyway." She looked furtively around, checking to make sure she was not in earshot. "This morning, we did a routine customs search of the Helios, just to rattle Xiang Zu's cage. An hour later, I'm hauled in to the chief and told to drop it or I'm out of a job. This came straight from the prince."

"I see," said Charles.

"So let me give it to you straight, Mr. Gardner. If you go on the record and submit that evidence, I'd give you about a week before you're dead and the evidence destroyed. Even if it wasn't destroyed, it would never get to court. In the meantime—you're still dead. There is no way this plays out where you're not dead. Except leave now—tonight!"

"I take it that you don't want the video then?"

"Is everything a joke to you?" She gave him a stern look.

Charles slumped back in his chair and looked out at the Helios again. "I wonder who she was?"

"It doesn't matter. If what you say is true then she's dead, you're alive—try and stay that way. Look, Charles... there was a time when I could do something, a time when I was a hero—I even have the goddamn medals to prove it. But not anymore. I have a young child to think of now. You know how it is. I have a different perspective on life." She stubbed her cigarette out under her foot.

Charles felt drained and he slumped back in the chair. "It's okay, I understand, I know what you mean. Things are different when you've got a family."

"Look, do yourself a favor and get out now, don't try and be a hero, you'll just end up dead."

Charles leaned forward, his arms on the table, hands clasped around his glass of champagne. "I can't leave now. Leonie's here for the Fusion Conference, that's a few days at least." He looked up at her and, almost apologetically, said, "I've really been looking forward to spending some time with her."

Madelaine leaned forward and put her hand on Charles's. "You have to go, before you get in way over your head, do you understand—you have to go."

He felt the warmth of her hand on his and, like the touch of a healer, it drained all the fight out of him. He let out a sigh. "Okay, you're right, I have to go."

She sat back in her chair, and the touch was gone. Charles felt intensely tired, not a physical tiredness but a kind of emotional weariness. He felt his body shake and fought hard to control it. "I'll go in the morning. I'll figure out something with Leonie."

Madelaine stood up and leaned over the table, her hand touched his shoulder. "I'm sorry there is nothing I can do Charles, really, I am. It's not fair and it's certainly not justice but I'm just... powerless." She turned to go.

"If you change your mind, about the video, that is, I won't be leaving until midmorning, by the time I get the boat ready."

"Goodbye, Mr. Gardner, and take care."

"Bye."

Charles knocked back the last of his drink. It was time to go. He was beginning to hate this place anyway. Overhead, a large insect buzzed, *zizz... zizz.*

15

BEFORE YOU DIE

They locked Marcel in a steel room in the bowels of the Helios, close by the engines. He knew this place, it's where you go before you die. It stank of sweat and blood and fear. This was where they had taken Marika. He thought he got the faintest scent of her perfume permeating through the foul air, but he could just be imagining it. He sat on the floor, hands tied behind his back around a thick steel pipe. For the first hour or so after they'd left him, he'd tried to free himself, but his wrists were raw from the effort. Eventually, when the pain got too much, he gave up.

For well over ten years, he had done Xiang Zu's bidding. He had been more than loyal, worked more than most, but it was not enough. Just when something good had finally prized him open and reached into his heart, it was snuffed out by Xiang Zu —and soon it would be his turn to be eradicated. He served no useful purpose now. He no longer entertained the master and had no place in the grand plan of Xiang Zu's ambition. Therefore, he must die. It had been decreed.

Yet he still had some time. They wouldn't kill him while the ship was docked in port. They would wait until it was out at sea and then he would be killed, just like Marika, with a bullet in the head.

There was no light in the small room, so he wasn't sure of the time of day, but he felt it must be late into the night. He tried to get comfortable and get some sleep. It was the only thing he could do.

Sometime later, he woke to the sound of gentle footsteps. A key turned in the lock, and the door opened very slowly and quietly. A figure, dressed all in black, entered and put his finger to his lips. "Shhhh." He knelt down beside Marcel, produced a knife, and proceeded to cut the ropes that tied his hands and feet. Marcel rubbed his wrists and shoulders to get some feeling back into them. The figure then lifted his balaclava up over his face. It was one of the old guys, Fredrick. He'd been with Xiang Zu a long time. When Marcel first entered the Xiang Zu empire, it was Fredrick that had taken him under his wing, showed him the way, and kept an eye on him.

"Fredrick... you're sticking your neck out for me?" he whispered.

"I owe you one. Remember when all that shit went down in Mauritania? They were going to slowly cut me up in little pieces and feed me to the pigs. You came back for me, Marcel, no one else did. You saved my ass. So I owe you."

Marcel gripped Fredrick's shoulder. "Thanks."

"Doesn't mean we're getting married." He winked and smiled. He pushed a bag into Marcel's hands. "Here, there's a wetsuit, gun, and some money." He unhooked a coil of rope from his shoulder. "You're going to need this too. There's security up on the stern, so you'll need to drop down the side of the ship somewhere into the water. You can make it over to the harbor without being seen if you're careful." He got up and opened the door a crack to check if all was clear. He took one last glance back at Marcel. "Be careful, and good luck." He disappeared out the door.

Marcel stood up, but his legs were cramped. He rubbed his thighs to get some feeling back, and, after a few minutes, he ventured a look out the door. The corridor was deserted. He stepped out, closed the door slowly behind him, and slid the bolt back in place. It was time to go. With a bit of luck, nobody would suspect anything until they entered the room to check on him. That wouldn't be until morning. So if he could get off the ship without being seen, then he'd have a good few hours to get as far away as possible.

The long corridor was dark and deserted. This part of the vast ship was seldom visited at night by anyone other than maintenance crew. It would lead him to the upper level of the engine room where there was a gantry ending at a service hatch in the starboard hull, his best escape option.

Marcel halted at the end of the corridor as it opened out into the cavernous engine room of the Helios. It stank of diesel and paint mixed with the smell of heavy machinery. Scanning the room as best he could from his concealed position, he listened intently for any sound of activity. He could hear the low hum of the generators, the background rhythm on any ship. It was a sound you learned to forget when you spend any length of time at sea, the constant background drone of motors.

Marcel quickly changed into the wetsuit and shouldered the coil of rope. He stuffed his clothes back in the bag and sealed it up good and tight. The Beretta M9 semi-automatic pistol he shoved inside the neck of his wetsuit and zipped it up. He moved silently across the steel gantry toward the hatch on the other side, all the while keeping his senses on high alert. Down below, the generators rumbled. He reached the hatch and was about to undo the bolts when he hesitated. A thought struck him.

This hatch was critical to the integrity of the hull when the ship was at sea, so it was possible that it might be alarmed. If it was, then it would sound an alert on the bridge. He considered this for a moment. Even if it was, it would still take them time to investigate, but eventually they would figure out he had escaped. He really needed as much time as possible to give him a fighting chance. Marcel stepped back. Maybe this wasn't such a good plan after all. His other option was to go up on deck and drop over from there, but it carried a higher risk of detection. But the possibility of setting off an alarm could mean game over for him. So he turned and headed back across the gantry and made his way up top.

Marcel poked his head out of the stairwell and scanned up and down the length of the starboard deck. It was dark and quiet at this time of night. His dark wetsuit helped conceal him in the shadows. The night air refreshed him, and he began to feel reinvigorated. Some lights were on toward the stern of the boat, but the bow was mostly in darkness. The other boats moored alongside also shared a similar paucity of illumination, with their bows mostly in darkness. He crept forward, keeping to the shadows, and over to the starboard railing.

He took the rope from his shoulder and was about to tie one end on the railing when he reconsidered. He would have no way to get it off again, and, once morning came, someone was bound to spot it. Nevertheless, it would still give him a few hours' head start. He peered over the railing and gauged the distance down to the sea below. He could jump, but the splash would be worse than an alarm going off.

He played out the rope through his hands and was pleasantly surprised to find it was longer than he thought. Even doubled up it was more than long enough to reach the water. That gave him an idea. He hung a loop loosely around a cleat and lowered both ends down into the water. He clambered over the railing, making sure to hold both ropes tight as he wrapped it around his torso and gently began to let himself down.

Voices.

Marcel stopped and listened. The ropes bit into his torso. He was no more than a few feet away from the bottom of the railing. He looked up and saw a guard leaning over. A faint blue glow of a vape illuminated his face. Marcel held his breath and tried not to move or make a sound. Then he heard another guard, somewhere further back, calling over to the man. They exchanged greetings and both moved off. He could hear their voices growing fainter.

Marcel slid down the rope as fast as he dared and slipped silently into the water. It was warm with a faint smell of diesel. He could feel it permeate through the wetsuit. He then pulled gently on one end of the rope. It slipped around its cleat and dropped down on top of Marcel. He pushed off into the hull to give him some cover as he stowed the rope over his shoulder.

Since all the boats were berthed with the stern to the harbor and brightly illuminated, he swam in the opposite direction where it was darker, moving from bow to bow until he eventually got to where the smaller sailing yachts were berthed. He swam slow and quiet, and kept close to the cover of the boats. After around a half hour, he dragged himself out of the water and onto a low marina walkway, quickly moving into the shadows. He took off of the wetsuit and got his dry clothes back on. To his enormous relief, the bike he had used earlier was still parked where he had left it. He began to breathe easier now that he was on dry land and had a way out. But he had just bought himself time, nothing more.

The question now, he thought, *is what do I do now?*

16

THE HELL OUT OF DODGE

What makes a person want to rise from slumber, to put one foot in front of the other and enter a new day? Is it desire, is it duty, is it hunger? Perhaps it is all of these, then again, perhaps it is none—just simply the natural order of things, the way things are, if you will.

Charles awoke.

He had no desire to rise, no desire to put one foot in front of the other—in fact, he had no desire whatsoever. What he did have, however, was an unmerciful hangover brought about by the consumption of way too much whiskey. He groaned. Then he remembered the previous night, the conversations, the dissolutions, the disappointments.

Inspector Madelaine Duchamp had abdicated all responsibility, chickened out, as it were. He thought about going higher up, but in reality that was just as pointless, so he had metaphorically closed the file on the case in his mind. He felt utterly drained. *How did it come to this?* he wondered. *How does it get to a point where nobody gives a crap anymore, at least not about anyone but themselves?* Then again, why should he give a crap? What made him so high and mighty to assume that anything he thought or did mattered to anybody?

But the real blow came when Leonie told him the channel had got them a spot in ITER, reporting live for the big event. It seemed that David's observations on the A team were correct, and they decided to do a *no show*. That left the channel in a tight spot. Not being at the science event of the century after having been invited would be disaster. So, Leonie and her B team were parachuted in at the last minute. The Fusion Conference here in Monaco was only a side show, after all.

They were dispatched last night and were now staying near Cadarache, across the border in France, for the rest of the assignment. A great career opportunity for Leonie, but hard on Charles who had been so looking forward to spending time with her. His only reason for mooring in Monaco was to spend a few days with Leonie. For weeks before it was pretty much all he thought about. Now even that had been denied him as well.

He felt he had lost his cardinal point, lost his compass bearing, so to speak. Maybe he was also losing his marbles. Then again, maybe he had lost them a long time ago when Jenny died. She was gone, his family was gone—making their own way in life. What was there left, this boat, this trip, this place? Was seeking retribution for the dead woman just a way for him to have some meaning in his pointless, indolent life? The thought resonated and echoed in his skull where it shocked him. What the hell was he doing here anyway, far away from home, far away from friends—alone. Loneliness enveloped him, wrapped him up like a blanket, sucked the will from his body, and deadened his soul. No, he had no desire to enter the day, not this day, not any day. The dark clouds had finally beaten him. He had no more fight to give—the battle was all but lost.

Then, in the darkness of his despair, a faint light glimmered, off in the distance, a mere mote in the blackness. Like a lighthouse in the storm, it pointed the way—he followed it. It grew and grew until it became a thought, and that thought was *home*. How long had he been gone, how long had he been running—too long. *Home*, he thought again. And, like a dead battery on trickle charge, the thought slowly gave way to desire, and desire grew into purpose—and purpose into action. He would waste no more time, enough of this place, enough of these people, he would go home. He rose from his bunk, perhaps just a bit too fast as a stabbing pain rifled through his brain. "Ohhhh..." he groaned as he lay back down. *Okay*, he thought. *I'll head home, just as soon as this goddamn hangover clears.*

By midmorning, Charles had gathered enough of his physical and mental self together to stand almost vertical and perambulate to the head—and promptly get sick. He prayed to God via the big white megaphone that was the toilet bowl. "Oh God," he said, repeatedly. After some time, God responded and gifted him the wherewithal to stand up, have a shower, and make a cup of tea. He was now sitting outside on deck, sucking in the fresh air, and sipping on the revitalizing beverage. He scratched his chin, finding it to be devoid of stubble for once. By the second cup, he was already doing a mental check of the boat, preparing to leave. He flipped the switch on the deck screen and brought up the systems check routines for all the mechanicals, then he went below and spent a few minutes doing a complete run through of all power systems. Battery bank fully charged, power generation steady at 6Kw, fuel at 73%, water at 94%. Then his mind turned to *where*? He brought up the navigation charts for this part of the coast on the main screen and checked the weather. An animated weather progression for the next twelve hours looped on screen showing wind direction and speed. *South by Southeast, Moderate.*

"So, where to?" he said to himself, examining the chart. "Antibes, that's about as much as I am up to the moment. Maybe push for Cannes if I make good time." He left the navigation table and headed up top, intending to do a full check of all gear. *Maybe just a quick check,* he thought, changing his mind. *Then it's time to get the hell out of Dodge.*

17

CHAMELEON

In the operations room on board the Helios, Mr. Wang hovered over his boss, rubbing his hands together like an anxious clerk. Xiang Zu cocked an eyebrow at him as he sat at his desk, amusing himself with his pet chameleon. Mr. Wang picked up a tablet, tapped it a few times, and a grainy video started playing on the main screen. It was a bird's eye view of two people at a café table. It had an eerie, night vision green palette. "The woman on the right is Inspector Madelaine Duchamp," said Mr. Wang.

They were looking at the video taken by the insect drone the previous night. Xiang Zu recognized the inspector.

"The guy on the left is one Charles Gardner. A lone yachtsman, small private boat. He moored in Monaco around the same time we did. What we have gathered so far from the recorded conversation is that he's the one who made the anonymous call to the police. And... eh, it seems he has a video recording of the event."

Xiang Zu raised his head and scowled at Mr. Wang. "What?"

"Fortunately, the inspector is not interested. It seems she's scared off," said The Patriot, who was relaxing on a sofa examining his nails. "Nevertheless, we are still keeping a drone on her, just in case she decides to be a hero."

"Do we know where it is, this recording?" Xiang Zu asked.

"We're pretty sure it's on his boat, on an SD card in his night vision glasses." The Patriot reached down to a pad on his lap and touched the screen, and a new video stream appeared on the main wall for all to see. It was a bird's-eye view from the top of a yacht mast. Down below, a slightly bedraggled looking man was sitting in the cockpit, drinking something and scratching his chin.

"One of the drones followed him back last night from the gallery and set up camp atop his mast."

Xiang Zu was now tickling the abdomen of his pet chameleon, and the exotic creature was doing a kind of weird dance, a step forward, then a step back, over and over again. A sort of rocking motion, like it was stuck in a loop.

"Should we kill him now?" offered Mr. Wang.

"Kill him, yes, but not here, not in Monaco. And we need to make sure the video recording is destroyed." Xiang Zu was now playing with something in his hand. It was a grasshopper.

Mr. Wang nodded.

"If he heads out of harbor, into open sea, can the drone follow him?" Xiang Zu placed the grasshopper on the desk.

The Patriot answered, "Better than that. It can stay with the boat and tell us his exact position no matter where he sails."

"Good, keep an eye on him. Once he leaves port, we can take him—out at sea. Make sure there is nothing left, no video, no boat, no Mr. Gardner. Got it?"

Mr. Wang nodded.

SLAP!

A flailing insect leg protruded from the chameleon's mouth as it chewed.

Xiang Zu smiled, again.

18

A STING IN THE TAIL

A gust of wind buffeted the tiny drone, causing it to increase power to its fragile wings so that it could maintain its track high over Louis II stadium—home of the Monaco Football Club. It had entered into an elliptical cross vector search pattern as it tried to locate its target, Inspector Madelaine Duchamp, who had disappeared somewhere in the crowd of people entering the soccer grounds a little earlier. Its cameras now scanned the multitude of faces on the stands and sent data back to the servers on board the Helios where fractal-based pattern recognition algorithms processed the information looking for a dominant percentage equivalence—otherwise known as a match.

It was easier to follow a target once the drone had a fix on them. By using predictive inference modeling, it could extrapolate the direction and speed of the target and literally keep one step ahead. However, that was a fat lot of good to it at the moment, as it needed to locate the target first. It was time to get serious. Since it now had no need for visual depth of field, it released its dual super hi-res cameras from stereoscopic duties and split them up to scan individually. All it required now was raw visual data so the servers could do their job and find the target.

"But Mom, you promised."

"I know Leon, I know. We'll go to McDonald's after the match, I promise."

"Okay, thanks, Mom."

Madelaine ruffled her twelve-year-old son's hair affectionately.

"Stop that, I'm not a baby." He patted his hair down again, sucked on his drink, and took in his surroundings. He could barely contain his excitement. "This is so cool. Do you really think they will win?"

"Oh, of course they will." In reality, Madelaine didn't know much about soccer. But according to Leon, Monaco FC were the best team, and were second in the French league, and if they beat Toulouse in the next match, they would be top of the table, and Valdez, their star striker, was the best player in the whole wide world.

However, what she was certain of was the delight in his eyes when she told him she had tickets for this special charity game this morning and he could bring his best friend, Pascal. It was not one of the big-league games, which was why she'd managed to get tickets for it, but this didn't seem to dampen the boys' enthusiasm. Madelaine sat back and took in her surroundings, the sound, the people, the anticipation—it felt good to be a mother for a change.

She had no great interest in soccer, nor any sport for that matter, but she had maintained a passing acquaintance in it for Leon's sake, as he had become a fanatical supporter over the last few months. She supposed this was probably a good sign, the sort of thing young boys do.

As they watched the game unfold, Leon and Pascal kept her informed of the brilliant play by Monaco, and especially Valdez. "See how he just went past those two guys. He's the best player in the world."

She agreed.

The game had been underway for around twenty minutes when her phone vibrated. It was an email from Maria.

As requested.

Madelaine opened the email.

Attached background on the handsome gentleman you were chatting up last night ;-)

Madelaine rolled her eyes to heaven. "Why does Maria have to constantly see the world through the lens of a teenage soap opera?" Nevertheless, it suited her purposes to let her think this —for the moment. She had asked for a background check on Charles Gardner without telling Maria why she wanted it. Just her luck that Maria had seen them in the gallery, put two and two together, and came up with five. She opened the attachment. It was a long PDF document, and it seemed that Maria had put *Marital Status: Widower* as item number one on the list. His wife died three years ago, cancer. There was more: children, education, residences, and so on.

Then it got interesting.

He was an electronic engineer and owned a security systems company in London specializing in covert surveillance. Primary clients included MI5 and MI6. He retired four years ago to sail around the world with his wife.

So he lost someone too, she thought. She knew how that felt. Her mind went momentarily to the Embassy in Bamako, Mali, and that fateful day when her life was torn asunder. She put the thought from her head and focused back on the dossier.

He was reported to be the developer of the *rock bug,* a clustered surveillance device and network node, miniaturized to look like a stone or small rock. Several of these could be scattered in an area and would interconnect wirelessly, intercepting phone data and monitoring movements. They were discovered by the Russians all over the Kremlin courtyard in Moscow and traced back to MI6. A huge diplomatic kerfuffle ensued.

It seems there's more to you, Mr. Gardner, than meets the eye, she thought. And, in a way, it explained a lot. That's probably why he wanted to do something when he witnessed the murder. He was the guy with the tools to gather the data but not the *Jason Bourne* that went out and took action. *Well, neither am I, dammit. I'm not the CIA, I'm just trying to keep my head down, well below the parapet.*

At the bottom of the file was a photograph, timestamped just a few hours ago. It was a still from one of the cameras overlooking the harbor boardwalk showing an empty berth where the Ave Maria had been. *So he's gone,* she thought. *Well, that's that.*

Then she did something she hadn't done for a very long time. She switched her phone off and stowed it in her bag. *Just forget it, it's over.* And went back to watching the game.

A palpable air of anticipation had been building in the crowd all around her. It looked like Monaco had got a corner and were ready to take it. The ball curled in over the front of the goal, and someone got a head to it. It went straight up in the air and came back down into a sea of frantic players. It bounced and bobbed and ricocheted around like a pinball. Eventually it came down to Valdez, about twenty meters out. He controlled it with his chest to direct it onto his right side, then he connected with a powerful shot and sent it straight through the knot of bemused defenders and into the back of the net. GOOOOOOOAL!

The crowd went mental.

Leon and Pascal were also going crazy. "I told you, I told you, I told you. He's the best player in the world." Madelaine agreed.

High up, inside the stadium roof, a small drone watched its target standing up on the seat, waving her arms around in the air and mouthing something along the lines of MON-AH-CO, MON-AH-CO.

19

OLD HABITS DIE HARD

Water lapped along the hull of the Ave Maria as it chopped a course through the northern Mediterranean Sea. Charles had taken it out from the busy Monte Carlo harbor under engine power, but, once clear of the main traffic, he hoisted the sails and cut the motor. It was a moment he always enjoyed, as the wind filled the canvas and the boat responded, heeling over to leeward before the magic of aerodynamics took over and the craft surged forward. It gave him a deep sense of freedom, a sense that the world was his to explore, a feeling that only a sailor truly knows.

He was now several nautical miles out from Monaco and had deployed a full main, jib, and staysail. Standing at the deck helm, he worked the sails to balance the boat on a steady six knot course, heading west-south-west toward Antibes. The deck navigation screen plotted his course, and, when he was satisfied all was okay, he switched on the autopilot. The system now took control of the boat, adjusting the rudder as needed. It took inputs from wind speed, GPS location, radar, and detailed navigation chart data. It would sail the Ave Maria all by itself to whatever coordinates Charles set. He left the deck and headed down below.

After making a hot mug of tea, he sat down at the navigation table and powered up his laptop. Using a secure Tor browser, he logged in to an encrypted server he kept for storing private data. He navigated to a directory timestamped the day before and selected a number of files with random sixteen-digit file names. He downloaded and decrypted them, then opened one up—it was an audio file. He hiked up the volume and listened.

The previous afternoon, when Charles had returned from his disconcerting expedition to paint *people* down by the main harbor, he had sat for some time in his tiny workshop contemplating his painting of the Helios. Beside it on the workshop bench was the card given to him by the Asian woman, Lao Bang. He looked at them both for quite a while, occasionally sipping from a glass of whiskey and ice. By the time he'd finished his drink, he had made his decision.

He grabbed a small power driver and headed into the yacht salon and proceeded to unscrew one of his paintings off the wall, bringing it back to the workshop. It took him a few minutes to check if the new painting would fit in the frame—it did—so he popped the back off and took out the old painting along with the glass. The frame was made from thick painted wood, and, using a small Dremel tool, he gouged out a long narrow track on the inside of one strut. He blew the sawdust away and examined it. *That should be big enough,* he thought. With that, he started to root around the workshop storage drawers, eventually pulling out a small bubble wrapped package and placing it on the bench. It was one of the many items he had accumulated over his many years in surveillance and simply couldn't bring himself to part with. So it all ended up on his boat because, *you never know when something might come in handy.*

It was a state-of-the-art surveillance bug, tiny and virtually undetectable. Unlike most bugs, which were simply radio transmitters, this used the GSM network. It would record audio for around an hour then compress, encrypt, and send the resultant file as data through the standard phone network to a secure server. It would do this once an hour, every hour until the battery ran out, which by Charles estimated was around three days.

He slotted a fresh SIM card into the bug and dropped it to the new groove in the frame. He then put in the new painting along with thick cardboard backing. He cut a rectangle in the middle of the cardboard to accommodate the tiny lithium-ion phone battery, right in the center so it wouldn't feel heavier on one side. Finally, he replaced the back and taped it up. It looked and felt pretty good.

That evening, en route to the art exhibition, he dropped into the office of a bike courier company in Monte Carlo and gave them the package to deliver to *Lao Bang, The Helios*. He had the card stuck to the front and thought no more about it until now.

He was about halfway through listening to the first file, but so far there was nothing to be heard. For the most part, it was just background noise, a low hiss. Yet every now and then he would hear disembodied voices, muffled and indistinct. He wasn't surprised by this. He clicked the stop button, opened the directory again, selected all the files, and dropped them into an audio editing program. The files opened one by one showing the entire audio waveform of each. If any of them had any data, then he would be able to see the peaks and troughs. The first two files had nothing at all, however, on the third and fourth it looked like he had picked up something. He clicked on the spot where audio seemed loudest and let it play.

He immediately recognized the Asian woman's voice. She was giving the painting to somebody.

"I have a present for you."

Charles laughed to himself. *Well I'll be damned.* Who the somebody was Charles couldn't be sure, but there was a good chance it was none other than Xiang Zu. There then followed a rustling and bumping as the package was unwrapped. Charles couldn't quite make out what was being said but he did catch the words *artisanal naivety.*

Pompous asshole, he thought.

The rest of the recording was pretty good, and Charles

could make out a fair percentage of the dialogue. The conversation wandered around for a while and then focused on some guy called Marcel. Whoever he was he seemed to have *escaped*. The rest of the conversation seemed to be about *the operation*, whatever that was.

He stopped the file and went to the next one. About two thirds of the way in, there looked to be a lot of audio so he started there. This was much louder, multiple voices, background conversations. It sounded like an operations room. The dialogue was very technical, with a lot of data being relayed. He caught phrases like: *activation, remote control.* There were others he didn't understand like: *codac, Mare Nostrum.* He also heard ITER being mentioned more than once. Charles listened for a while to this seemingly incomprehensible babble. However, one voice began to stand out. It was very matter of fact, almost sarcastic. He talked like he was translating all the technical jargon for someone else in the room.

The device has been activated, we can take full autonomous control when we're ready. They won't even know it until it's too late, then... oh no... bang go the cryogenics and ka-boom... bye bye ITER... kiss my ass!

"Holy shit," said Charles out loud.

He moved the audio head to the start and played it again. He turned the volume up and listened very, very carefully. By the third pass through the audio file he was in no doubt.

They're going to sabotage ITER. He was sure of it. *Right at the point of ignition. Leonie is there, I have to warn her, tell her to get the hell out!*

He jumped up from the navigation desk and fished his phone out of his pocket and hit her number. *Sorry, but the person you are calling must have their phone switched off or are not in range...*

Damn! She probably can't get a call in the main ITER control room since it's a high security area. However, he had one other hope, albeit a slim one. He hit number for Inspector Madelaine Duchamp. *Sorry, but the person you are calling must have their...* "Bollox!" he shouted into the phone. He was on his second *bollox* when there was a massive jolt to the starboard side of the boat and it sent him flying across the salon floor.

"What the...?" He got himself together and headed up the companionway to the deck. He was just coming through the hatch when he saw three armed men in a powerful rigid inflatable boat, a RIB, one of whom was climbing over the side railing.

Pirates? In the Med? Holy shit! he thought, just as the intruder swung his body around and kicked him hard in the chest. Charles went straight back tumbling through the companionway and landing badly on the floor below. "Ahhhh..." He had just enough time to lift his head and see the butt of a gun as it connected with his temple. Pain seared through his head as he contorted in agony. He felt himself being dragged into the center of the salon. He was hauled on to the seat and the man had one hand on his neck and the other pointed a gun at his head.

"Where's the video?"

"What?"

He whacked him again with the back of his hand. "The recording you took of the Helios, where is it?"

Charles struggled to comprehend, the pain blinded him. "Recording?"

"WHERE'S THE VIDEO?" he raised his gun butt again to strike.

Charles acquiesced. "Laptop... it's over by the laptop."

"Show me." He dragged Charles up from the seat and pushed him over to the navigation table.

It was the video of the woman's murder they wanted. *How the hell did they find out?* he wondered. At least it seemed they hadn't found the bug in the painting—for all the good that was. He closed the audio program just in case and reached for his binoculars. He extracted the SD card, inserted it into his laptop, and opened the file. "There," he said.

"Okay, you sit quiet now, over there." He jerked the gun at the galley table. Charles hobbled over and sat down. *How the hell did they find out?* he thought again. He looked over at the navigation table. The huge guy was watching the video and laughing.

"Happy?" said Charles.

"Ha, ha. Very happy."

Another guy then poked his head down though the companionway and spoke. "Mr. Wang, are we good?"

"We're good, and as soon as this asshole is dead, we'll be even better."

"Go fuck yourself," said Charles.

"Ha, ha, brave man. But soon you'll be one dead dickhead." He got up and moved over to where Charles was sitting and whacked him again hard across the temple with the butt of his gun. This time, Charles's world went dark.

20

THE OLD MAN AND THE SEA

Charles was neither awake nor asleep, neither conscious nor unconscious, and it was at these times that Jenny would come and talk to him. She was sitting across from him, the sun's rays illuminating her face which was crowned by a broad brimmed pink sun hat, she was reading a book.

"Hello, Charlie," she said.

"Jenny... am... am I dead?"

"I don't think so, Charlie."

"What are you doing here?"

"Oh, I'm just reading a book, *The Old Man and the Sea*. It's about a sailor who bites off more than he can chew."

"Yes, I remember it. That sounds like me, doesn't it?"

"It does, Charlie. And it seems you've got yourself in quite a pickle."

"I know."

"Are you going to save Leonie?"

"Save Leonie... save Leonie?" he pondered this question. It was significant in some way, then he began to remember.

"There's no way out, Jenny, no way out. I can't even save myself."

"That doesn't sound like the man I knew. He would always find a way. That's what I loved about him, he would always find a way."

"That man is gone, gone a long time ago. He died when you did, Jenny."

"My poor Charlie, you have to let me go, you need to think about Leonie, she's what's important now."

"Leonie?" he struggled to make sense of his thoughts, to make sense of his surroundings. Yes, Leonie was in danger, what could he do, there was something urgent—what was it?

"You have to let me go, Charlie, and find Leonie."

"Yes, I do, I need to... find Leonie... that's what's important... Jenny... Jenny?"

He opened his eyes very slowly. Bright sunlight penetrated his brain, and with it came a dull, throbbing agony inside his head. He looked for Jenny, she was gone—so he let her go. Slowly he gained some physical awareness, and with it came more heightened pain. He groaned. He was lying face down on the floor of his cabin in the Ave Maria. He tried to move, but his hands and feet were bound. His head hurt something serious. He felt the hum of the engine through the floor of the cabin.

Where the hell are they going? he wondered. Then his

thoughts turned to Leonie and the plot to sabotage ITER. *What time is it now? Do I have any time left?* Maybe it didn't matter as he would probably be dead pretty soon, and if their plan for ITER succeeded then probably Leonie be dead too. He had to try something, anything.

They had obviously reefed in all the sails and were now under engine power, heading full speed to wherever it was they were going. Judging by the sound of the engine, they were pushing it full throttle. Charles could see the sun out the port side window. So they were heading south, far out into the Mediterranean. The sun was still high, so he must not have been out for very long—maybe he did have some time.

He tried to free his hands, but they were tied tight together behind his back. Then he tried to reach into his pocket, where he kept his sailing knife. *A sailor should always have a knife on their person in case they should be tangled in rigging and be at grave personal risk.* It was a line he remembered from some old sailor's handbook. It was very good advice since he was now pretty tangled up and *at grave personal risk.* He contorted his body and dug deep into his pocket. He could feel it with the tip of his fingers, but it was a struggle to get both hands in while bending backward with a throbbing head. He was beginning to feel a cramp coming on in his back. He relaxed, stretched his body as best he could and tried again. This time he managed to capture it between his two index fingers and carefully pull it out enough to grab it with one hand. He unfolded the blade and started to saw through the ropes. He then freed his feet, stood up, and stretched his muscles. He felt his temple. It was caked with blood, his hair matted into it. It was painful to touch.

The door to the main salon was slightly open and he peered through the crack. Lying on the main cabin lounger was the monster they called Mr. Wang, holding an automatic weapon across his massive body. He looked like he was sleeping.

Charles gripped the knife firmly in one hand, so much so that his knuckles had turned white. It was extremely sharp with a serrated edge and could be a vicious and deadly weapon—in the right hands. But Charles wasn't so sure he had those hands. Could he rush into the cabin and drive the knife into Mr. Wang's throat? Look him in the eye as he died and say something like, "Who's a dead dickhead now?"

But he knew he couldn't do it. He couldn't kill someone, even if that someone who was going to kill him. He just didn't have it in him. And even if he could, what about the other guys? There was at least one manning the helm and another one in the RIB. He doubted he could get further than a few steps before he died in a hail of bullets.

"Dammit, think!" He whispered to himself as he looked at his watch. There were still a few hours before the ignition test at ITER. He still had time. He searched his pockets. His phone was gone, dropped in the salon when the RIB hit. He peered through the crack again looking around and saw it lying on the floor, hidden behind the table strut. If he could get his phone, then he might have a chance.

Just then Mr. Wang moved, scratched his forehead, and sat

up. Charles stepped back from the door but could still just make him out. He was getting up and walking toward the companionway. He climbed the steps and out on deck. It was his chance. It was now or never. Fear gripped him. He hesitated. Should he go and get the phone? Doubt crept in. Would they hear him? He opened the door and was about to move when he saw Mr. Wang's feet coming down the companionway steps. He closed the door over again. *Dammit,* he thought.

Mr. Wang had a bag with him this time. He put it down on the galley counter, opened it, and took out what looked to Charles like a quarter pound of butter. *He's not going to start cooking, is he?* Charles wondered.

The next item he took out of the bag Charles recognized instantly. It was a remote trigger device. So the quarter pound of butter was probably C4 or Semtex or whatever the hell was flavor of the month in *Bomber's Quarterly*. Charles was no expert on explosives, but he still knew enough to know that the *quarter pound of butter* probably wasn't enough to blow the Ave Maria sky high. But it would be enough to blow a massive hole in the hull and down the boat would go, with him in it. Minimal debris, nothing to find—he would be just another *lost at sea* statistic.

Charles watched as Mr. Wang assembled the bomb. Then another guy shouted down through the hatch, "Ready? RIB's here."

"Yeah, just a minute." Mr. Wang stood up and checked the remote trigger. Satisfied, he left the salon and went out onto the deck. Charles reckoned he would then transfer onto the RIB, and when they were all far enough away, detonate the bomb—bye bye, cruel world.

The main engine stopped, and the boat jolted as the RIB came up alongside. Charles knew he now had only moments to live. Faced with the inevitability of his imminent demise, all fear evaporated from him and in its place was simply the will to live.

He dashed for the galley as he heard the RIB's engines power it away. His heart was pounding, but adrenaline kept the pain in his body at bay. He looked at the bomb. "Think," he said to himself. He knew very little about bombs other than there was always uncertainty about whether to cut the green or the blue wire.

"Don't get giddy. Just focus." He took a deep breath.

"Battery, circuit board, detonator, quarter pound of butter." He identified each component. "Long wire from the circuit board... radio controlled... anti-tamper?" He considered for a beat, then said. "Screw it."

He pulled the battery from the board. He was still alive. He pulled the detonator out of the *butter*. He was also still alive. He threw the detonator into the steel sink and stood back. He had done it, he wasn't dead—now what? He rushed over to the window and looked out. The RIB was stopped a good distance from the yacht and by now they were probably wondering why the bomb hadn't gone off. He had bought himself some time, nothing more, soon they would be heading back to investigate. However, this time he would have a little surprise for them.

During the planning stages of his sailing trip, he had for a while considered taking the Suez Canal down through the Red Sea and out into the Gulf of Aden. But it was a dangerous route with Somali pirates roaming the Arabian Sea. So he had rigged up a quick and dirty electric fence. He had stripped the insulation from the stainless steel wire railing all around the deck of the boat. Then he wired it to a bank of very large capacitors. He could, in theory, charge these up and with the flick of a switch send a very unhealthy fifty thousand volts through the wire and anything touching it. Not enough to kill someone, possibly.

He hit the button and heard the telltale squeal of the capacitors charging, a sound not unlike an old-fashioned electronic flash. It took a minute or two to get fully charged, so he looked out the window again. The RIB hadn't moved. *Still some time,* he thought. Then he had an idea. "You just never know when some of that *stuff* might come in handy," he said to himself.

He dashed into his workshop and started frantically pulling out drawers. "Where the hell is it? I know I have some somewhere." He dumped the contents of the drawers all over the floor and started rummaging through it.

"Found it!" He held aloft a bubble wrapped package, like a miner who just uncovered a diamond encrusted rock. He grabbed some tools from the bench and dashed back to the galley where the disassembled bomb lay and started to reassemble it. He had found a small radio controller trigger with a simple radio-controlled switch and was now wiring it up.

His hands were shaking, sweat dripped from his forehead. He tried to calm himself. "Don't mess this up... stay focused... breathe." He hastily reassembled the bomb without blowing himself up and was now, very, very, very carefully, putting it inside a watertight plastic food container when he heard a buzzing noise.

Zizz... zizz.

It sounded like a very large insect, coming from outside on deck. He slowly climbed the steps and peered out the door. At first he couldn't see anything, so he climbed another step, then another to get a better view.

It came out of nowhere, swooping down from above the boom and hovered right in front of his face. It looked like a giant dragonfly. "Holy crap!" He slammed the door shut just as the drone spat at him. A row of darts hit the woodwork above his head before it closed, he threw the bolt and stood back. "Insect drone." He could see it through the porthole, buzzing around outside. He studied at the metal darts stuck in the woodwork. They were stainless steel needles with what looked like a black ooze covering the tip. "Poison darts. My god." Here was state of the art drone technology married to primitive botanical wisdom. *What the hell sort of Frankenstein machine is this?* he wondered. Yet, however much Charles's moral fiber was repulsed at the creation of such a mechanical abomination, his technical brain marveled at the brilliance of it. Standard munitions were way too heavy for these tiny drones, but poison darts—that was genius.

Through the side window of the yacht, he could see the RIB cautiously working its way toward him. They obviously knew he had escaped, but also knew that he was trapped below deck. His plan had involved being up on deck when the RIB came in, but the deadly insect drone hovering around outside meant that was no longer an option.

What to do, what to do? he thought, as he franticly tried to come up with an idea. Maybe he should just wait until they were all on board, detonate the bomb and take the bastards down with him. It was an option, and he was fast running out of any others.

The buzzing of the insect drone stopped.

He looked out the porthole in the hatch and saw that the drone had perched itself on the deck railing. It was looking in his direction, so he gave it the one fingered salute. "Say hello to my electric friend," he said as he flicked the switch for the electrified railing.

The drone exploded into a thousand pieces.

Bits of it rained down all over the place as he reset the railing charger. Charles then opened the door and crawled out on deck, keeping as low as possible. He started the engine and pushed the throttle a little forward. There was absolutely no way he could outrun a fast RIB, but he wasn't going to make it easy for them either. Gunfire erupted and bullets ripped through the side of the boat. He crouched down, covering his head as he was showered with wood splinters and debris. They were obviously getting a bit pissed off with him. Under a hail of bullets, he crawled back to the salon and fell down the steps. The gunfire stopped and the RIB hit the side of the boat.

Charles poked his head up just as Mr. Wang grabbed the railing. He flicked the switch again and an unholy scream emanated from the massive Mongolian. He was flung back into the RIB, hitting the driver, and sending the RIB careering off course. Charles rushed out on deck and flung the bag with the bomb onto the bow of the RIB. He jammed then throttle fully forward and turned his boat to starboard to get some distance. He was lying flat on the cockpit deck when he took the trigger out of his pocket. He couldn't see how far he was away from the RIB, but he didn't care anymore. "Okay, you bastards. Let's see what you think of this." He pressed the button.

The force of the blast hit the side of the Ave Maria and Charles was sent flying across the deck. He thought it was going to roll all the way over, but it came right again, and he was sent tumbling back to the other side as he was showered with a deluge of water and debris. Wreckage banged and thumped off the deck for what seemed like an eternity. When it finally stopped Charles cautiously raised his head above the deck. The RIB was gone, in its place was just a sea of wreckage. He slumped back down and finally allowed himself to breathe. He glanced at this watch, four and a half hours to ignition.

With an aching body and throbbing head, he struggled to stand up. No time to waste. He turned the yacht north, back toward land. Then he heard the bilge pumps kick in to clear the boat of sea water. But something wasn't right, the boat felt heavy. He was taking on a lot of water. The explosion must have

GERALD M. KILBY

damaged the hull. He rushed downstairs and looked at the bilge meter. It was climbing up and the pumps couldn't get it out fast enough. It was the moment every sailor fears—he was going to sink. It was inevitable. It wasn't a matter of *if*, simply a case of *when*.

"Dammit, and it was all going so well." He shook his head.

21

MAYDAY

"Mayday... Mayday... Mayday. This is sailing vessel Ave Maria in need of immediate assistance...over." Charles lifted his thumb off the VHF mic and waited for a response.

The speaker crackled back. "Sailing vessel Ave Maria this is Nice Coast guard, what is your situation...over?"

"This is the Ave Maria, hull damaged and rapidly taking on water. Estimate ten to fifteen minutes before I sink. Will deploy life raft shortly and activate personal locator beacon...over."

"Sailing vessel Ave Maria, message confirmed. How many persons on board?"

"Just one."

"Be advised, coast guard helicopter on its way to you shortly."

"Message confirmed. Ave Maria out."

Charles rushed to a locker beside the main cabin and started pulling on boots and a sailing jacket, over which he put a life vest. The cupboard was also where he stored his *grab-bag*. That essential bit of kit that every sailor should have in case you ever needed to ditch. He then rushed around the boat grabbing essentials, passport, wallet, phone. "Phone, where's my phone?"

He found it after a minute. The face was smashed. He tried to power it on, but it was dead. He shoved it in his pocket anyway. Lastly, he grabbed his laptop and stuffed it into the grab-bag and sealed it up. Water was beginning to slosh around his ankles as he ran up the steps. Then he remembered something and went back down the galley where he opened a storage locker and took out a full bottle of 27-year-old Redbreast Irish Whiskey. "I'm sure as hell not leaving this behind."

As he headed back up the companionway steps, he spotted the poison darts still stuck in the woodwork. He stopped and very carefully pulled them out one by one, placing them into a small Ziploc plastic bag he grabbed from the galley. He rolled the bag up tight and put it in a side pocket of his jacket. He wasn't sure why he was doing this, maybe it was morbid fascination, maybe it was as a memento of this whole episode— something to remind him of why he was losing his boat.

There was no more time to waste. He ran to the quarter deck and kicked the straps off the life raft cocoon. He pulled out the lanyard and clipped it to the railing, then pushed the cocoon overboard where it split open and self-inflated. He pulled it back in against the hull, unclipped the lanyard and jumped into the center. It took him a few seconds to find his balance, but, once he did, he pushed off from the side of the Ave Maria with his feet and collapsed back into the raft.

For some time, he sat back and watched the stricken vessel as it succumbed to the sea. First the stern dipped below the water, then slowly the rest of the boat disappeared, leaving only the mast descending like a submarine periscope retracting into the depths. When the last trace of the Ave Maria finally went under, Charles was filled with a strange mix of emotions. His boat—the boat he had poured his energy into over how many years, the boat that he and Jenny had planned to sail around the world on—was gone. In a way, it was his connection to her, and now that connection had been severed. There was a sadness, but also a release. It felt like a physical snap as he watched it go down. He slumped down in the life raft, and his body shook as he let go of all his pent-up emotions.

Suddenly, the raft dipped violently on one side as a hand came out of the water and grabbed the rope. Charles scrambled to the opposite side of the raft, trying to regain some balance as Mr. Wang's head appeared over the edge. He hauled himself into the raft, coughed and spluttered, and looked over at Charles.

"Ha, ha... *cough...* thought I was dead, did you? I see your boat's fucked." He glared at Charles for a moment with the look of someone on the edge of reason—and then he lunged.

"Bastard. You're gonna die for sure this time." He grabbed Charles's neck in an iron grip, choking him. Charles turned and twisted and tried to pull his hands away, but Mr. Wang was demoniacally strong. He felt his throat being crushed. He couldn't breathe. He tried thumping him in the ribs, but he couldn't get any leverage. He tried grabbing his head, then his eyes, but he was too slippery.

Then he remembered the barbs in his pocket. It was a long shot. Charles reached in, slid out the Ziploc, and rammed it into the side of Mr. Wang's neck. Mr. Wang shrugged. "Ha, ha... you'll need to do better than that." His hands tightened again, and Charles twisted and turned and fought with all his remaining strength. But he was beginning to lose focus, his body becoming starved of oxygen. But, just when he had given up hope, Mr. Wang's grip loosened, and Charles grabbed a gasp of air. Then, Wang's body relaxed, his eyes rolled up in his head, and he collapsed down on top of him. Charles mustered up enough remaining strength to push him off, just before he, too, finally blacked out.

22

LOST AND FOUND

"Come on, there's a free table over there. Try not to knock anybody down on the way." Madelaine balanced the tray of food, picked her way over, and sat down. Leon and Pascal began re-enacting highlights from the soccer match with animated detail, in between scoffing down a celebratory chicken mc-somethings and coke. "And then he went... *whack*, and it was the best goal ever."

"Yeah, and did you see how he went around those two guys?" Pascal then proceeded to demonstrate using some conveniently placed chairs as defenders.

"Settle down, Pascal. Eat your food." He was a nice kid, but a bit on the hyperactive side for Madelaine's level of childminding experience. If he was a criminal, she could just handcuff him to something that didn't move, like a railing.

Crime was so much simpler to manage than children. But soon hunger got the better of them, and they settled down.

They were sitting at tables outside the shopping center of Fontvieille, looking out across the street at the small harbor lined with sailing yachts and smaller boats. Madelaine checked her watch and scanned the crowd. They were to meet Pascal's father, Anton, here after the match. It was handy, near the soccer ground, and relatively inexpensive. At least in this place feeding two kids didn't break the bank. This was still Monaco, after all. Madelaine spotted Anton making his way through the crowd, and she stood up and waved him over.

"Hi, how was the match?" He strode over.

A riot of gesticulation and exclamation ensued, with both boys trying to outdo each other with descriptive awesomeness.

"So it was good then?" He sat down at the table.

Part of Madelaine envied his ease with the boys, maybe it was a man thing or maybe it was just his way—nothing was ever a hassle. She didn't know that much about him, just that he was young and handsome, and he was Leon's best friend's dad. It seemed the only people she got to meet was through Leon. Without the school gate ritual, she probably wouldn't meet anyone anymore. She wasn't sure what he did and there was never a mention of a mom—maybe he was a weekend dad. However, every time she met him, she found herself worrying about her hair, her clothes. It was stupid and she knew it, but she just couldn't help it.

"Wow, two nil. Valdez is the best player in the world," said Anton.

"The best," agreed Leon.

"Thanks for bringing him to the match," he said to Madelaine.

"No problem, any time." She pushed an errant lock of hair away from her face and smiled brightly, then realized what she was doing—too late, damage done. She felt like a schoolgirl.

"Dad, can Leon come over for a swim in the pool, please, please?"

"Well, you'll have to ask his mother." He looked over at Madelaine.

"Oh, eh... I don't know."

"Please, Mom. Please can I go?"

"Well, I suppose it's okay, why not," Madelaine acquiesced.

"I can drop him back later," said Anton. "It's no problem."

"Thanks. That would be great."

Anton stood up. "Okay guys, ready to go?"

They jumped up from the table. Leon gave his mom a hug, and all three headed off leaving Madelaine alone with the mess. She watched them as they made their way through the crowd and out of sight.

She sat there for a while sipping her coffee, not really sure what to do. She was alone with her thoughts, and, for the first time in a very long time, she had nothing to do—it felt very weird. She lit a cigarette.

There were tricks she had learned to keep the memories at bay. These she had developed into an ad hoc set of rules. Rule number one: stay busy. Rule number two: never be alone with nothing to do. She had just broken her first two rules, not by desire but simply by events. An anxious wave rippled through her. She took a long drag from her cigarette.

For a time, she simply watched the drift and weave of the people as they moved around the shopping center concourse. Mostly tourists, backpackers, families on a budget—happy people, not a care in the world. They chatted and laughed, enjoying the sunshine and each other's company. She stubbed her cigarette out in the little tinfoil astray and considered lighting another, but stopped herself. "I really need to give these things up," she said to herself. Instead, she sat quietly and sipped the remains of her lukewarm coffee.

The plaza was bordered by a thick low wall topped with planters that screened the al-fresco diners from the traffic on Avenue Albert II. Here and there along its base were little alcoves for water pipes and access to horticultural whatnots for the maintenance of the foliage. From one of these alcoves, down at her feet, and for no reason she could explain later, she felt something looking at her. She gazed down, and from the darkness within she could just make out two tiny eyes peering up at her. It gave her a start and she shifted in her chair. When she looked back, they were gone.

She kept very still and peered at the space with intent. Sure enough, the two little eyes reappeared. They were too big to be a rodent. Maybe a cat then. She very slowly took some of Leon's unfinished chicken and tossed it down in front of the alcove. A small bedraggled-looking dog stuck its head out and scoffed it down in a flash. She broke off a bit more but this time she held it in her hand.

"Here, little doggy. Want some more?" she said in a low, singsong voice. It poked its head out a little, but wasn't sure. Hunger moved it forward, but fear held it back. She dropped the morsel. It wolfed it down and retreated again. Madelaine offered it another. This time it ventured further and accepted it from her hand. Madelaine could see it was pretty beat up, its left ear was matted with dried blood, and it seemed to hold its back leg up as it hopped forward. It must have been at the wrong end of a fight with a cat or another dog maybe. However, it did have a collar with a tag, so perhaps it was lost. By the fourth morsel of chicken, she had gained enough of its trust to pick it up. It shivered and its heart raced. It was very frightened. "There, there now. Let's have a look at your tag."

Fluffy.

"Well, I'll be damned."

23

RATTLING CAGES

Inspector Madelaine Duchamp burst through the front doors of the Monaco Harbor Police station like a medic shepherding a traffic accident into emergency surgery. She spotted Maria over at her desk and made a beeline for her.

"Guess who I found?" The little dog was in the process of licking her ear when she plonked it down on Maria's desk.

"Don't tell me it's Fluffy-Wuffy." Maria looked a bit closer at the dog as it stood shivering in fear at the strange environment. "Or at least, what's left of it."

"Yes, she's a bit banged up, aren't you, you poor thing." Madelaine tickled its chin. It reciprocated by giving her another lick.

"Eh... what do we do with it now?" Maria was not a dog person.

"Give it some food and water... plenty of water, and get it to a vet. Then give the Princess a call and tell her the good news. No doubt I will be awarded the highest honor in Monaco for such a service to the state."

"Water, right, okay... eh... what do they eat?"

"Well this one seems to like chicken nuggets."

"Should I send out for a takeaway for it then?" Maria's brow contorted into a question.

"You're really working blind on this one Maria, aren't you?"

"Sorry, don't know much about dogs."

Fluffy was now chewing Maria's stapler. "Tell you what, just call Sargent Jules from the dog squad. He'll know what to do, and they can look after it over there for a while."

"Of course, yes." She went to pick up her phone. "Eh... does it have to stay on my desk until then?" Fluffy had now moved on to her pen holder and was making short work of it.

"Yes, would you mind?"

"Well... er..."

"It's a joke Maria. Here, I'll take her in to my office, you call Jules."

"Oh, ha... Yes... will do."

Madelaine picked the little dog up in her arms. It snuggled in.

"Oh, did you get my message earlier on?"

"What message?"

"About your sailor friend, Gardner. He sent out a Mayday from his yacht around an hour ago."

"What!"

"Yes, I messaged you about it."

Madelaine put the little dog down on the desk again and rummaged through her bag. "Damn, I switched my phone off."

"You did what?"

"Yes, well I was... I mean, I am on leave." She pulled the phone out of her bag. "Is he okay?" she asked as she switched it on again.

"I don't know. They sent a rescue helicopter out from Nice General. That's where they'll take him."

"Sorry, Maria, can you sort out the dog for me? I need to go talk to the chief." She dumped the little dog on the desk again and raced off down the corridor.

By now, Fluffy's digestive system had done all it could with the chicken nuggets and the little dog twisted and turned on Maria's desk. Finally, nature took its course and it squatted on its hind legs and laid down a bad boy all over Maria's nice clean paperwork.

"Agggghhhhhhhhh..." said Maria.

"And you say he has video evidence?" Régis Onassa leaned back in his chair and considered Madelaine for a moment.

"He does," replied a breathless Madelaine.

"You're going to be opening up a whole bag of trouble for yourself running after this one." He sighed, "Okay, but be subtle about it. You go and interview him, you get it on the record, and for God's sakes make sure you have it in the bag before you go rattling any cages."

"Thanks, Chief."

"Don't thank me yet. First you need to find out if he's still alive, then if he'll talk, and then if he still has the recording. That's a lot of ifs."

"It's worth a shot. After all, it's what I'm paid to do." She turned to head out the door.

"And Madelaine."

"Yes?"

"Be careful."

She nodded. "I will." And left the office.

Okay, she thought. *I should take a chopper. That's the quickest way to get to Nice General Hospital.*

Overhead, as Madelaine made her way to the Harbor Police heliport, a small insect drone kept a very tight bead on her.

24

SWARM

A grainy image of Charles Gardner giving the one fingered salute from the Ave Maria was frozen on the main screen in the operations room on board the Helios.

"This is the last image just before the drone went dead," said The Patriot. "A short time later, Gardner instigated a Mayday call from his yacht. When the rescue chopper finally arrived, there was no sign of his boat. However, they did pick up two bodies from a life raft and brought them back to Nice General. We don't know yet who they are or if any of them are still alive."

Xiang Zu massaged his temples.

"Also," The Patriot continued, "Inspector Duchamp just lifted off from the police heliport a few minutes ago, en route to

Nice. The drone that is keeping an eye on her has attached itself to the chopper, so it's traveling with her."

"I have seen that face somewhere before." Lao Bang's head was enveloped in a cloud of cigarette smoke. She waved it aside.

"I did some quick research on this guy, and check this out." The Patriot tapped a few keys and a document appeared on screen. In one corner was a photograph of Charles Gardner, in the opposite was the MI6 insignia. "It seems he's a retired electronic surveillance expert, formally contracted by British Secret Service."

"Any word from Mr. Wang?" Xiang Zu asked, still messaging his temples.

"Nothing so far."

"I recognize that face?" Lao Bang jumped up from her seat and walked over to Xiang Zu's desk. She picked up the painting she had given him the previous night. "He's the street artist, the guy who did this painting." She held it up for all to see. They stopped, looked at the painting, and then back at the screen.

Xiang Zu grabbed the painting from her and examined it, turning it over and back. Finally, he ripped the back from it and a small lithium-ion battery fell out. Everyone stopped and looked at it.

"Is that what I think it is?" said Lao Bang.

Xiang Zu continued to dismember the picture frame until he finally pulled out a small electronic bug. He held it up and looked at it.

"Oh shit," said The Patriot.

"I'm beginning to really dislike this individual. I want to know where he is, if he's still alive, and then I want him DEAD!" Xiang Zu thumped the desk. "And whatever recording he has needs to be destroyed. So take a chopper, some men and whatever resources you need, and get this mess tidied up once and for all."

"Absolutely," said The Patriot.

"NOW!" exclaimed Xiang Zu.

The Patriot headed out of the operations room and as he did, he considered that this was the perfect opportunity to try out *The Swarm*. He smiled to himself. *This was going to be a whole lot of fun.*

25

THICKER THAN WATER

Charles was neither awake nor asleep, neither conscious nor unconscious, and it was at these times that Jenny would come and talk to him—except this time she didn't. Instead, it was a burning cocktail of fear and urgency that welled up inside his subconscious, and, like a shot of adrenaline to the heart, it kickstarted him into the waking world. He sat bolt upright in the hospital bed, eyes wide open, and scared the shit out of the nurse that was keeping an eye on him.

She jumped up, knocking over her chair. "Oh my god," she exclaimed, holding a hand to her heart.

"What time is it?" he croaked.

Before she had time to recover and answer, several hospital staff rushed into the room and massed around Charles's bed. They assumed the standard medical detachment honed by years of procedural training. "Mr. Gardner, how are you feeling?" said a portly doctor as she poked a light pen in his eye.

"Fine, fine." Charles croaked again and looked at the clock on the opposite wall. *Still time,* he thought.

"Mr. Gardner, I'm Inspector LeMon." An official-looking identity badge was thrust in his face by a tall thin man with a rather hang-dog expression as he squeezed through the medical melee. "I need to interview to you about what happened."

Charles looked at it. "Yes, sure, absolutely."

"Privately," said LeMon to the head doctor. She grumbled about *checks* and *tests* and *procedures,* but eventually she left, followed by her medical entourage.

Charles looked at the inspector. "Listen, this is very important. I have evidence of a plot to sabotage ITER during the ignition test, today."

"I see," the inspector replied a little skeptically. "That's very interesting."

"We don't have much time, the test is in less than four hours' time," Charles urged.

"Indeed." The inspector took out a notepad.

Charles sighed. *This is going to take forever,* he thought.

"Inspector, get me my laptop, I have all the evidence you need on that."

The inspector smiled and nodded calmly. "Yes, but why don't you just tell me in your own words, starting with what happened out on the water." The inspector sat down beside the bed, opened a blank page in his notebook, and clicked his pen.

Charles let out a long slow breath. "Okay, Inspector. The way I see it is like this. There's the hard way or there's the easy way. Let me outline the hard way first. I jump out of bed, strangle you with my bare hands, run out of here in this hospital gown with my ass hanging out, steal a car, drive to ITER and get gunned down ramming the gates, while screaming out for my daughter, who is, as we speak, reporting from inside ITER for a major news channel. End result is you die, I die, my daughter dies, and probably a load of other people die. Now, that's the hard way. The easy way is to get me my laptop, okay?"

Inspector LeMon looked at Charles for a minute, sighed, and unclicked his pen. "Fine, I'll get the laptop."

"Thank you, Inspector."

It took Charles a full twenty minutes of explaining and cajoling and pleading before Inspector LeMon was finally convinced that the threat to ITER site was real, or at least real enough to act. Charles popped an SD card out of his laptop and handed it to the inspector. "Here's a copy of the recording. Please get this to your Intelligence Agency and get that test stopped or the consequences could be catastrophic."

"I'm not making any promises. Frankly, it all seems very peculiar," said LeMon as he folded closed his notepad and headed out the door.

Charles could still see the inspector through the glass wall that faced out on to the long corridor, talking to a police officer and looking over at Charles as they spoke. Yet something seemed to be the matter with the officer. He was grimacing and clutching his neck. The inspector looked concerned and put a hand on the young office arm just as the officer's legs gave way, and he collapsed on the floor.

Charles jumped out of bed, ripped off all the wires that seemed to be attached to him, and raced over to the glass wall. He could now see the officer feebly pulling something from his neck and examining it. It looked to Charles like a fine steel needle with a blackened tip. Then the officer went limp.

LeMon suddenly pulled his gun and started moving back along the corridor, a look of horror on his face. Then a small insect drone came into view, similar to the one that Charles had electrocuted back on board his boat.

That thing is after me, he realized. *How the hell did it know I was here?*

Inspector LeMon fired off a shot with a shaky hand and missed. Medical staff screeched and scattered. LeMon edged further back down the corridor. The drone advanced.

Phhit... phhit... phhit...

Several steel barbs punctured the skin on LeMon's face. He fired off another shot, more desperate this time. The drone dodged and kept advancing, spitting out more of its deadly needles. LeMon fell to his knees, then slumped over on the ground. The drone hovered above him, presumably checking to make sure he was no longer a threat. Once it was satisfied that Inspector LeMon was incapacitated, it rose up, turned, and faced-off with Charles on the far side of the glass wall for a beat. Charles instinctively moved back a few steps, even though he was pretty sure the drone couldn't get in. But how was he going to get out?

Suddenly, the door at the far end of the corridor burst open and several uniformed guards burst in. The drone flicked around to face them, hovered for a moment, then flew off in the opposite direction. Presumably it decided there were too many for it to take on. Charles reckoned it was his opportunity to get out—but not before putting some clothes on.

He was searching for his belongings when that door to his room swung open and in raced Inspector Madelaine Duchamp, pistol in hand. "Madelaine, what the hell are you doing here?"

"It's okay, Charles. Just stay calm. Everything is under control."

"Trust me, Madelaine, everything is not under control. There's an insect drone on the loose out there, very nasty, extremely dangerous." He was getting dressed as fast as he could.

Madelaine shut the door and began looking this way and that through the glass as the other guards moved off down the corridor.

"Are you sure? How do you know?"

"We've met before. Anyway, that's beside the point. Tell me what you're doing here? Last time we met I was under the impression you didn't give a crap."

She turned back to face him. "I met a dog."

"A dog?"

"It's a long story." She gave a dismissive gesture.

Charles began stuffing his laptop into the grab-bag he took

from the sinking boat. He still couldn't quite contemplate the thought of his beloved yacht at the bottom of the Mediterranean—but all that mattered now was Leonie.

"And here was I thinking you were a just lonely, melancholic gentleman with a passion for art." Madelaine continued. "Now, apparently, you're a lethal weapon."

"Are you talking about what happened out at the boat?"

But before she could answer, Madelaine jerked her pistol up and backed away from the glass wall. On the far side, the drone had returned.

"It's here! Outside," she exclaimed. "What the hell does it want?"

She raised her gun to shoot.

Charles moved over and stayed her hand. "Careful, they're very fast, hard to hit. If you miss, then the wall is gone and it will be in here spitting death. Just wait, let's think."

The drone moved off down the corridor again, presumably looking for another way in. Madelaine reluctantly lowered her weapon.

"I uncovered a plot by Xiang Zu to destroy ITER during the test today."

"You what?" Madelaine gave him a startled look.

"Yes, things have moved on. It's no longer about the murdered woman."

"How did you find out?"

"I bugged his boat," Charles replied with a sly smile.

"Why does that not surprise me." She shook her head.

"It's what I used to do, it's a long story."

"I know, I read your file, *Inventor of the rock-bug*."

Charles gave a laugh and shrugged his shoulders apologetically. "The problem is, they must know that I know about the plot. Maybe they found the bug, or maybe that insect drone somehow overheard my conversation with the unfortunate Inspector LeMon, who knows. The upshot is ITER goes boom today unless we can stop it. And there's one other thing. Leonie is there reporting for the channel."

"Oh..." Madelaine began to realize what was at stake.

"Yes, like I said, things have moved on a bit since we last met. In the meantime, that drone wants me dead before I can get this information out." They both looked over at the glass wall.

"Have you got a phone?" Charles asked.

Madelaine reached for her pocket. "Crap, no. I left it in my bag."

"Who else is out there?" Charles looked up and down the hallway trying to see any signs of life.

"Just hospital security staff, they're probably searching for it, or maybe they decided to wait for the police."

"Or maybe they're already dead."

"Either way, we should just sit tight. The police will be on their way."

"Don't be so sure. Someone has to be operating that drone, so there are real people with real guns somewhere out there, and by now they're probably heading our way. By the time the police get here, it will be too late. We need to get out of here now." Charles hefted the grab-bag over his shoulder and was considering just making a run for it when the drone reappeared again on the other side of the wall. But before Charles had time to react, Madelaine raised her gun again and took careful aim.

"Looks like there's only one way out of here. Cover your face," she said in a low voice, just before she fired.

The glass shattered into a thousand pieces with a deafening crash. She inched her way forward, keeping the pistol high. On the floor outside, the drone buzzed and crackled, its delicate wings destroyed by the flying glass. Madelaine took aim, fired, and the drone exploded into a thousand pieces. "Let's get out of here."

They raced down the corridor and pushed through the door to the stairs. Madelaine took a quick look over the railing. She snapped her fingers and motioned for Charles to follow her. They ran down the stairs, through the ground floor doors, and out into the open.

"This way, come on." She rushed ahead. Charles followed and soon realized they were heading for a small white helicopter with the Monaco Harbor Police insignia emblazoned on its side.

"You have a helicopter?" Charles surveyed the machine.

"It's a perk of the job."

"An actual helicopter? I'm impressed."

"Just get in. Quick."

He climbed in. Madelaine pointed to a headset. "Put that on." She began flicking switches and the chopper powered up, then lifted off as she pulled back on the stick. They rose over Nice General Hospital and headed east toward Monaco.

"Get me to ITER," said Charles.

"What? But that's miles away. We need to get to Monaco and report everything. They'll alert ITER."

But from Charles's experience with the skeptical Inspector LeMon, he wasn't so sure that they would be treated it with any urgency. "Call it in on the radio. And tell them we're heading to ITER. Leonie is there, I need to warn her and get her out."

Madelaine considered this for a moment. "If what you say is true, then that could be really dangerous, suicidal even."

"You don't have to stay, just get me in there. You can get me in, past the security. You can land in the facility, you've got the clearance."

There was a silence from Madelaine.

"Look, Madelaine, she's my daughter, the only thing I really care about in my life. My wife is gone, my boat is gone, and my old life is now a distant memory. She's the only thing left in this world that matters to me. I have to get her out, I have to try —please."

Madelaine gave him a long, considered look, then turned the chopper north toward Cadarache. "Okay," she sighed. "But I must be losing my mind."

26

HAVING A BAD DAY

The helicopter weaved its way north toward Cadarache, hugging the contours of the southern French countryside. Charles could see its shadow dancing along the rolling hills of vines and lavender. Madelaine had radioed in and explained the threat to ITER. So it seemed that the wheels of state security were finally kicking into action. The test would be stopped, and the crisis averted. Charles began to relax.

His body still hurt from the encounter on the water, and as he touched the bandage on his head, he felt a throb of pain. He was battered and bruised, and his mouth felt dry and foul. He reached behind the seat for his bag and rummaged through for a bottle of water, taking out his laptop to get at the bottom of the bag. He was about to put the laptop back when he decided to listen to some more of the recordings from the bug he had planted. There was still another twenty minutes before they got to ITER, so he had time. He stuck in some earbuds under the chopper headset and plugged them in to the computer. He listened for around ten minutes, skipping and jumping around the audio files. He heard phrases like *autonomous control, facility lockdown, cryogenic event failure.* Each one of these phrases added to a disconcerting queasiness that was fermenting in his gut.

Some of the dialogue seemed to be about the *device* they were using to control the mainframe. He got a sense that they had achieved some deep level access to the ITER systems. Charles was beginning to think that it might not be as easy as just shutting down the test. He pulled the earbuds out and turned to Madelaine.

"Have they canceled the test yet?"

"I'm not sure, there is a lot of confusion going on down there. I haven't got positive confirmation back yet."

"What about Leonie, did they get the people out?"

"I don't know," she looked at Charles. "Don't worry, I'm sure it's all under control."

"How much longer?"

"About five minutes."

The uneasy feeling was building in Charles. ITER may be *under control,* but whose control was the question. He looked out the helicopter window again, he could see its shadow rolling along the ground. It reminded him of one of those old shadow puppet theaters, telling tall tales of gallant knights on crusade, or maybe Don Quixote fighting windmills. It was the way the shadow undulated with the topography, in and out, up and down. It was hypnotic and calmed his simmering anxiety.

Then a second puppet entered the theater a little further back—it was bigger and cast an ominous shadow over the dainty French countryside. It advanced with each undulation.

"We've got company," he finally said.

"What?"

"There's another helicopter behind us." He jerked a thumb over his shoulder.

"It's not one of ours." Madelaine gave him a concerned look, shaking her head.

With that, glass and debris exploded all around them as chopper was raked with bullets. The machine banked hard to the right and went nose down as Madelaine fought to control it.

Charles' head bounced off the side window. "Arghhh!"

Madelaine slammed a foot on the dashboard and pulled on the stick with both hands.

"Come on you bitch, pull up, pull up." The chopper slowly leveled out.

"Where the hell are they?" They heard more automatic fire, but none hit the chopper this time, as far as they could tell.

"Over there, over there." Charles shouted. "Look, that's ITER. Can you get us down?"

Madelaine maneuvered the chopper toward the facility, pushing it as hard as she dared. But another burst of automatic fire raked the machine, sending more shrapnel flying around them. The chopper jolted, followed by the screech of grinding metal from somewhere deep in the mechanics of the distressed machine. Smoke started to fill the cockpit, lights flashed, and warnings beeped, the chopper vibrated and whined—the noise was deafening.

Smoke burned Charles's eyes as he flipped open the side window to get some air. He began to cough and splutter.

"Come on, don't give up now." Madelaine wrestled with the stick. Sweat dripped from her forehead, her shirt was saturated. "Mayday, Mayday, Mayday. This is Inspector Duchamp, Monaco Harbor Police. Goddammit! The radio's gone. Okay, hold tight. I'm going to kill the engine."

"What?"

"Trust me. If I don't, it might explode."

"Don't we need it to... like, stay up?"

They were almost over the ITER compound now, down below Charles could see security people, paramedics, emergency vehicles, all looking up at the stricken helicopter. The vibration was now so bad Charles felt his fillings were going to pop out.

"Here we go." Madelaine killed the engine. The chopper dropped out of the sky with a gut churning plunge—Charles felt as if he was going to throw up. Around ten meters from the ground, Madelaine pulled hard on the stick, the machine went nose up and slowed down dramatically. The rails hit the ground and skidded with a demonic screech of metal for twenty or thirty meters, then stopped.

"Holy shit," said Charles.

"Out, out, out—now!" screamed Madelaine.

"What—?" Charles opened the door and fell out of the

chopper. He held his side trying and moved as fast as he could toward a cluster of ground crew. He got maybe thirty meters when the chopper blew up.

The shockwave walloped him in the back, and he lifted off the ground for a brief moment before hitting the hard concrete pad with a thump. He rolled and rolled, and finally came to rest lying on his back staring up at the sky.

His head buzzed and his hearing was shot. He caught only the muffled sounds of paramedics shouting at him. The smell of smoke and burning oil filled his nose and mouth. He felt dizziness and pain. Then the ground crew were around him lifting him on to a stretcher—their heads blocking out the sky.

"Madelaine?" His voice was a hollow croak, he coughed. Someone gave him water and he drank, pouring the rest over his head, the cold sting revitalizing him.

"Madelaine, where's Madelaine?"

"Ee-ine-ee-kay," came the muffled reply.

Charles couldn't hear, his head was just a dull whining whistle. He rubbed his ears. The paramedic gave him the thumbs up. She must be okay then. He was pushed back down on the stretcher by the grinning paramedic who kept giving him the thumbs up. Having just survived a helicopter crash most people would be more than happy to lie back and take it. But Charles didn't have that luxury, if you could call it that. He grabbed the thumb happy paramedic by the cuff.

"Has the ignition test been stopped? Are the people out?"

"Eh-ee-ka," was the response.

He lay back down rubbing his head as they manhandled

him into the back of a waiting ambulance. When the gurney clicked into place Charles tried to swing his legs over the edge and sit up. But Mr. Thumb was having none of it and gently pushed him back down. Charles signaled for some water, raised himself up on one elbow, and gulped down half a bottle. The act of swallowing seemed to make his ears pop and he sensed his hearing improving. He let out a long sigh. He was just about to interrogate Mr. Thumb again when Madelaine showed up, bruised, battered, and bloodied—but still operational, more or less. She was also on a gurney, she looked over at Charles. "You okay?"

His ears seemed to have rebooted and, while not quite a hundred percent, were at least ready to fight another day. He raised the bottle in his hand.

"Still alive. By the way, thanks for the lift, sorry about your helicopter."

"It's okay. I can get another one," she smiled and grabbed the bottle of water from him.

"Speaking of helicopters, any sign of our friends?" asked Charles, as he massaged the side of his head.

Madelaine took a couple of swigs of water. "No, they're not going to get too close to here, too much firepower on the ground."

The ambulance stopped, the back doors opened, and Mr. Thumb insisted they lie down again. "Just until we get you inside and checked out." He and the other crew ushered them out of the ambulance and into an attendant melee. They wheeled them into the medical facility and parked them up in the main clinic. Madelaine swung her legs over the side of the gurney and stood up. "Sorry, but you'll have to lie down."

She raised her hand. "I'm fine." She walked around a bit.

"Sorry, but I must insist."

"I said I'm fine, so back off." There was a bite to her words.

They backed off. "Can we at least take a look as those scratches?"

She felt her shoulder. Her shirt was torn and bloodied. She sat back down on the gurney with a groan. "I suppose so."

The medic moved toward her slowly, like she was some sort of wild animal that could turn and take a bite out of him. Charles had to admit, she had a way about her that commanded respect, perhaps even a little fear. Perhaps there was military there somewhere in her background, or maybe she was just having a bad day.

Now that Madelaine had taken the lead, he swung his legs over and stood up. Bad move—he lay back down again, his ribcage hurt like hell. She was obviously made of stronger stuff.

"Inspector Duchamp." A stocky military commander burst in through the doors followed by two heavily armed gendarmerie. "Jean-Luc Bastion, Chef d'Escadron" He had an impressive array of military insignia. "What the hell happened up there?"

"We encountered direct small arms fire from sources unknown, the transport was compromised so I had to execute an EHL."

It struck Charles that Madelaine had to have had some

military training in a previous life, or else she spent a lot of hours on a PlayStation.

"You're damn lucky to be alive." He grabbed a chair, swung it around and sat down facing Charles with his arms resting on the back. "Mr. Gardner?"

Charles nodded.

"Tell me everything you know."

27

THEN IT EXPLODED

I t was late morning when Marcel finally opened his eyes and looked up at the canopy of olive tree branches above him, dappled sunlight danced across his face. The previous night, after setting off from Monaco, he was not sure of where to go or who to trust, so he simply headed west toward Nice. He drove as far as he could before sunrise, and, as the first dawn rays were beginning to brighten in the sky to the east, he turned north into the hills. The land changed to scrub, then thick groves of olive and lavender, then to woodland. Marcel turned off the road, found a spot with the best cover and settled down to rest and think. Ten minutes later, he was asleep.

He awoke some hours later feeling surprisingly refreshed, but, better yet, he knew exactly where he should go. He would go home—something that he should have done a long time ago.

He rose, brushed the dust from his clothes as he mounted the bike, and drove out of the woods back down the mountain toward the coast. He kicked down a gear on the Ducati as he leaned into the corner. The motorbike glided through the bend like it was on rails. He powered out, twisting down gently on the throttle, the engine raising in pitch as he increased the revs. Flipping over on the seat, he dropped back on the throttle as the bike banked into the next corner and gracefully flowed through. The road then straightened out after the journey down from the winding mountains. With each passing moment, he could feel the air getting warmer around his body. He twisted hard on the throttle, and this time the engine screamed in response as he accelerated up through the gears. Power surged through the machine—he was at one with the bike—he felt good.

Marcel always had a sense of being connected with the world when he was on a bike. Cars insulated you from the environment, even with the top down. In a car you simply traveled past, never really experiencing the journey through the place. No real sense of presence, no tactility. To Marcel, it was like traveling through space wearing bubble-wrap. A bike, on the other hand, put you slap bang in context. The wind, the smell, the movement. You were hardwired to the place, a high-speed sensory location dump. There was nothing like it.

He was now on the main motorway through the mountains and heading southwest toward the sea. The road was now a dead straight four lane blacktop for the next sixteen kilometers. Marcel pushed the bike hard. The tachometer red-lined and the speedometer hit one eighty, he was going fast. Being at one with the bike was a transcendental state, where mind, body, and machine were locked in blissful harmony. However, it did have its downsides, especially when one's mind is racked with emotional turmoil.

The bastard had killed her, his Marika. Xiang Zu looked her straight in the eye and put a bullet through her head. He had taken away her life and left a gaping hole in Marcel's soul. Up until now, Marcel hadn't realized he even had a soul, and he wished he didn't, as his body, once more, shook with rage. The speedometer hit two forty when he was overcome with a burning desire to clutch the cross around his neck, his hand left the drop-grip before he realized what he was doing.

Too late—he was no longer at one with the bike.

Had there not been a piece of shorn truck tire on the road at that particular moment, he probably would have been all right —but life's not like that. The bike bucked, then shook, then wobbled before Marcel finally lost control. His brain was now firing on all cylinders and time slowed down. *Stay with the bike, stay with the bike,* he thought. He gripped the machine as tight as he could as it dropped and slid, sparks flying out from the crash bars as it skated along the road. *Stay with the bike, stay with the bike.* It spun around and around, and he lost all sense of position. *Hang on, hang on.*

After what seemed like an infinity of spinning around, the bike hit the crash barrier at the side of the motorway with such force that Marcel was wrenched from the machine. He found himself in midair flying over a fence into a dry scrub field. *Roll.*

When I hit the ground, roll. He hit the ground, he rolled, he kept rolling, and rolling, and rolling, and then, when he stopped rolling, Marcel's world went dark.

At the side of the motorway, the mangled bike dripped fuel, its wheels spun, its vitals hissed—then it exploded.

28

MARENOSTRUM

There's an old nineteenth century church, Torre Girona, nestled in the grounds of the University of Catalonia in Barcelona, Northern Spain. It is unique among churches. Not by virtue of some architectural oddity nor any singular artistic endeavor, not even because it now accommodates a very large gleaming glass box. No, it's because inside that church sits what is arguably the world's most beautiful supercomputer—MareNostrum 5.

Where once penitents came to genuflect before its altar and seek forgiveness for their sins, now scientists come before the great machine to seek answers to the mysteries of the universe. Where once the faithful brought offerings from nature's harvest, now physicists offer up datasets and algorithms. Where once there was blind faith, now there is simply science.

The brooding magnificence that is MareNostrum 5 was

currently using a fair percentage of its 204 petaflops of computing power to process and respond to a multitude of data streams now entering its buffers from the International Thermonuclear Experimental Reactor, ITER. It blinked and hummed with cybernetic satisfaction as it rendered the information through its silicone substrates.

ITER had its own mainframe, CODAC, a powerful system in its own right, but a poor relation to the awesome processing power of MareNostrum 5. So, extensive use had been made of the supercomputer during the development phase to model and test the complex engineering and physics inherent in ITER's creation. More recently they started to run full ignition test simulations in real time, ironing out the kinks, tweaking the systems, and feeding back into the final startup sequencing that was to run on its own in-house mainframe. However, running a full simulation on MareNostrum was not part of the ignition test plan. The two systems were not connected, so there was no way that the supercomputer could actually control ITER.

Dr. Stephanie Perdomo sat at her terminal looking at the surge in activity on the central cores on one of Europe's largest supercomputers. She tapped a few keys on her terminal keyboard to bring up a summary of the datasets it was processing. After scanning the list for a few minutes, she picked up the phone and hit one of the extension buttons.

"Juan, sorry to bother you but there's just been a massive spike in CPU load."

"Oh... yes, I forgot to mention it to you. You know ITER is

running the ignition test today... the big *save the world* moment, they just wanted a bit of extra reassurance from Mama Mare."

"But Juan, this is not scheduled. This is highly unorthodox."

"It doesn't matter, we can bill them for the extra time."

"But who authorized this?" She was not letting it go.

"Stephanie, it's fine. Just let it run and don't mess with it, okay?"

She thought about this for a moment. "All right, if you say so." She reluctantly agreed.

"I do."

She put the phone down and went back to her terminal. It was a religious holiday in Spain today, so most of the staff were off. It was just herself and Juan monitoring all the running processes, which made this current test all the more odd. If ITER had planned using MareNostrum for an ignition simulation, then there would be at least another half dozen staff. *What the heck is going on?* she thought as she brought up a list of all running processes on screen and started to delve deeper. Then she noticed something she had never seen before in all the ITER simulations she had been involved in. She picked up the phone again.

"Juan, sorry to bother you again but there is something very strange going on here. It looks like MareNostrum is negotiating two-way coms over TCP with CODAC."

"It's fine, just leave it alone."

"But Juan, this is weird. Maybe I should call the director and get some more data on this."

"No, for God's sakes, don't do that."

"Why not?"

"Eh... it's a holiday, don't go disturbing him when he's spending some time with his family. Just leave it be."

"Well okay, but it's all very strange." She hung up again, but this time she had the distinct feeling that something was not quite right. Processes kept cascading down her screen, multiple TCP/IP requests—all very strange.

She picked up the phone again but this time she dialed the director's private number. She held the receiver to her ear as it rang... once... twice. Before it got to the third ring it was yanked out of her hand and placed back on its cradle.

"I told you not to do that."

"Juan, what the hell are you doing?"

"Look, Stephanie, I like you, you're a nice girl. I would hate for anything to happen to you, I really mean that."

"Juan, you're scaring me. Maybe you should just back off."

"All you had to do was leave it alone, but no, you had to start fucking things up."

Stephanie got up from her seat and grabbed her bag. "I'm just going to leave now, Juan."

He grabbed her by the arm. "I'm sorry, Stephanie, but I can't let you do that."

She kneed him in the balls, and he dropped like a sack of stones. "Go screw yourself, creep." She made for the control room door. But before she could get there, a large insect dropped down from the ceiling and hovered right in front of her face. She screamed and stepped back. It looked at her—she looked at it. There was a momentary stand off before Stephanie swung her bag at it, but it moved too quick.

It spat, *phitt... phitt... phitt...*

Two barbs stung her face, another one penetrated her left eyeball.

"Noooooo," yelled Juan from the floor. "Don't kill her, she'll keep quiet. Please don't kill her."

Stephanie swung wildly with her bag, not sure where the thing was.

Phitt... phitt...

Two more barbs embedded in her arm. She felt weak, she stumbled, a blurry image of the drone hovered in front of her face—she collapsed on the ground.

Juan managed to pull himself upright again and looked down at the prostrate form of Dr. Stephanie Perdomo.

"You bastards, it was just for the money, nobody was supposed to die." He turned and sat down at one of the terminals. "Well, you can go and screw yourselves." He started tapping the keyboard to disable all the rogue processes.

Phitt... phitt...

"Agghhh," he pulled the barbs out of his neck.

Phitt... phitt... phitt...

He dropped to the floor.

The drone then ascended into the confusion of wires and ducting that was the control room ceiling, attached itself to a power cable, and observed the two bodies on the floor as their lives slowly ebbed away.

29

CONTROL ROOM

D avid panned the camera in a long sweeping arc around the inside of the ITER control room, a gigantic bunker on two decks accommodating a hundred or so engineers, physicists, and scientists—known collectively by all at ITER as *fusioneers*. The entire back wall of the control room consisted of a screen festooned with data visualizations and video feeds. Down on the main floor, circular groups of workstations radiated out from a central dais like petals on a flower. David finished his pan, dropped the camera from his shoulder, and turned to Kats, who was consulting her clipboard. They were on the upper deck along with a small gathering of the world's top news media.

"Can you believe this place? It's like NASA meets IKEA."

"Yeah, it's pretty amazing. Okay, we've got an interview in a few minutes with Professor Jason Manderbast."

David let out a laugh.

"What's so funny?"

"Manderbast. That's a helluva name to have attached to a human."

Kats shook her head, "Can you just for once try to be professional? We've got a serious job to do."

Just then, Leonie walked through the crowd of assembled media. With her was a tall thin, well-dressed man sporting a bowtie. David elbowed Kats and whispered in her ear. "I bet you it's that bastard, Mander."

She stifled a giggle and elbowed him back. "Will you cut it out."

Leonie was in full director mode. "Okay, I think we should do the interview over here, so we can have the main area in the shot. Can you cue us up Kats?" Leonie readied herself for the interview. David hoisted the camera.

"In three... two... one." Kats counted down with her fingers.

"Here we are today inside the incredible ITER control room where, later on, we hope to be witnessing one of the greatest scientific achievements of the 21st century. I am delighted to have with me Professor Jason Manderbast, one of the lead physicists here at the facility, to give us an insight into the fusion test that's taking place." Manderbast nodded at the camera.

Leonie turned to him. "Perhaps you can tell us a little about the significance of today's event?"

"Of course, always a pleasure to be talking with you. As you may know, one of the great challenges for humanity is clean energy supply. Our current reliance on fossil fuels is a concern both in terms of its effects on the environment as well as the sustainability of such resources into the future. A further concern is the ever-increasing demands for more energy as the world continues to develop. These are real and significant challenges for humanity as a whole. Fusion, on the other hand, has none of these issues. The fuel is Dutritium, an isotope of hydrogen, and found naturally in seawater, and we have plenty of that—two-thirds of Earth is covered in water. However, what we need is a working fusion reactor, something that has evaded the best minds and engineers for decades. Until today, that is. Very shortly we should have the very first truly sustainable fusion reactor. It will be a truly momentous occasion," said the Professor.

"Can you tell us a little of how the process actually works... I mean, what is fusion?"

"Good question, Leonie. Fusion is what powers the sun and every sun in the universe. It's God's power station, so to speak. So what we are trying to do here at ITER today is recreate that energy source, it's really a small sun in a box."

"So how is this achieved?" Leonie asked.

"With great difficulty." He laughed. "We heat the hydrogen fuel up to around 150 million degrees, many times hotter than the center of the sun. Once we get enough energy into the plasma, it will become self-sustaining. This is the magic that has never been done before in any meaningful way, and that's what we hope to achieve here at ITER today."

"Fascinating, Professor. Now, I have to ask the question on safety, but how safe is the process?"

"An excellent question, Leonie. There has been a lot of erroneous information circulating about fusion reactors. This is NOT..." He stabbed the air with an excited digit. "I repeat, NOT a nuclear reactor as most people know it. This is a common misconception, they are like chalk and cheese. Nuclear fusion is an inherently safe process, the by-product is helium. The best analogy I can make is that a standard nuclear reactor—a fission reactor, so to speak—is like trying to keep control of a nuclear bomb. A fusion reactor, on the other hand, is like trying to keep a match lit in a hurricane. The slightest thing and the reaction stops. That's partly why it's so hard to achieve."

Behind them, on the main control room floor, a ripple of activity radiated through the assembled *fusioneers*. Professor Manderbast looked across at the data on the screens.

"One last question, Professor." Leonie tried to refocus his attention back on the interview. But he seemed a little concerned by the data readouts on the main monitors.

"Sorry, but I think I need to get back now." He smiled weakly.

"Oh... okay, thanks for taking the time to talk to us."

"No problem, always a pleasure." He turned and headed off.

"Something is not right," said Leonie as she surveyed the mood of the assembled technicians and scientists.

"Don't be daft," said David.

"Look." She nodded toward the main floor where the activity had become visibly more animated. "They're not happy campers. And did you see the expression the Professor's face before finished the interview?"

"You're just being paranoid," said David. But he too was sensing the changing mood.

"Something's not right, I can feel it," said Leonie, as they all watched Professor Jason Manderbast sprint out of the control room.

30

LOCKDOWN

P hysical security had always been a major concern at ITER, as far back as its inception. This responsibility had been given over exclusively to France and the French military. They had full veto at the site. Any threat to security and they had the power to press the big red stop button —and the crash landing of a bullet ridden helicopter within the ITER facility certainly fit that bill.

Jean-Luc Bastion, Chef d'Escadron of the division in charge of ITER security, placed the intelligence document carefully on the conference room table, in front of a hastily assembled ITER directorate. He stood up, cleared his throat, and commenced.

"What we know so far is this." He looked at his watch. "Approximately thirty-five minutes ago, a Monaco Harbor Police helicopter made an emergency landing within the ITER facility. On board were Inspector Madelaine Duchamp and a civilian. Both sustained only minor injuries and that incident has been contained." He looked around at the group of shocked faces.

"However, we believe there is a significant threat to the security of the ITER reactor during the ignition test today." He glanced at his watch again. "As a result, we are suspending the test. All systems are to be taken offline immediately."

The directorate were stunned. They looked at one another with gaping mouths and elevated eyebrows.

"What sort of security threat are we talking about? Terrorists?" said Professor Asama, the ITER director general.

"I'm not at liberty to discuss the intelligence details. But I can say this. We know the threat is to destroy the reactor right at the point of ignition. But we don't know how this is to be accomplished. Nevertheless, by taking the reactor offline we eliminate the danger and secure the facility."

"This is incredible," exclaimed Professor Manderbast, as he studied a real-time camera feed of the main ITER control room displayed on a large wall monitor in the conference room. He could sense the confusion building between all the *fusioneers*. They were clustered in groups, talking, gesticulating. Clearly, they had just received instructions to down tools. *The media are going to have a field day,* he thought. *This is a disaster.*

The professor was still looking at the monitor when up popped the head of Fontella DeSilva, the control room director, on conference call. It was a direct video link and the red box around the image indicated it was a secure connection. She looked extremely concerned.

"Fontella," said Professor Asama. "I realize you must be very concerned with these security developments. But we have been assured the everything is... eh... contained. Nevertheless, it has been deemed necessary for the security of the facility to shut down the reactor and suspend the test. I know, I know, this is an unfortunate turn of events, but we must put security first. Can you give us a status report on the shutdown process?"

Fontella seemed flustered. "Eh... we seem to be having some, eh... technical issues. I'm sending you a process output stream now."

On the monitor a new window opened. Line after line of computer messages appeared with [DENIED] in bold red lettering after each item. A collective murmuring cascaded around the room as one by one the assembled directorship realized the implications of what they were seeing. It roughly translated as, *oh shit*!

"Can somebody tell me what is going on?" Jean-Luc, not being technical, couldn't interpret the screen. display but presumably he knew enough to know that [DENIED] was never a good sign.

"We are trying all protocols," said Fontella, a little breathlessly. "But the systems are not shutting down. It's crazy. It's like we're locked out of CODAC."

"Can't you just pull the goddamn plug?" offered Jean-Luc.

Before Fontella had a chance to respond to Jean-Luc's helpful suggestion, the control room filled with flashing amber light and a warning klaxon barked. Then a disembodied voice started announcing. *Caution, facility entering lockdown. Stay clear of the doors. Caution, facility entering lockdown.*

The directorate were on their feet now, eyes glued to the scene unfolding in the control room. "What the hell?" offered Jean-Luc. Nobody was sure what was happening, the entire directorate were in disarray.

"Fontella, why are we going into full lockdown?" Manderbast shouted over the rising voices.

The control room director shook her head. "The only reason is if CODAC detected a *central interlock violation.* But everything's still up and running. Everything *looks* normal."

"Except we can't stop the test," replied Manderbast.

"Wait a minute." Fontella looked down at some screen she was using. "That's funny."

"What? What's funny?" The professor prompted.

"Temperature fluctuation in cryogenics. That's what set off the lockdown routine. Weird, it seems okay now."

In the control room, huge concrete blast doors could now be seen sliding into position. The disembodied voice continued its cautioning—the news crews were loving it.

"Do you think you can you shut it down?" asked Jean-Luc.

"We're working on it."

"Okay, you've got ten minutes. If you can't shut down by then, we start an evacuation of the facility."

"What? You can't be serious!" exclaimed Manderbast.

"I have no other option." Jean-Luc shook his head. "Once ITER enters full lockdown, the security protocol dictates full evacuation."

"But..." Manderbast continued his protest.

"Ten minutes!" Jean-Luc shouted emphatically, then grabbed his papers and headed out of the room followed by his aide-de-camp. A stunned ITER directorate watched him leave.

Manderbast glanced around the room. It was chaos. *This is crazy,* he thought. With that, he quickly grabbed his bag, threw it over his shoulder, and ran out after the Chef d'Escadron.

By the time he'd caught up with him, they were outside the main HQ building. "Commander!" he called.

Jean-Luc turned, saw Jason, and raised his hand. "There's nothing more to discuss, Professor."

"What are you not telling us? What's the actual threat? We need to know, know now." Jason was panting from his exertions.

"Sorry, but that's classified, there's nothing more I can tell you."

"I don't think you understand what's going on here, the system is not under our control, you need to tell us what you know so we can try and get it back." The professor gestured wildly.

The commander clenched his jaw and swung around to face off with the professor. "I'll tell you what I understand, all personnel will be evacuated out of the facility." He stabbed a finger at Manderbast. "That includes you, Professor."

"What about those locked down in the control room, the technicians, the press people? They have no way out."

Jean-Luc didn't reply, he simply turned his back and walked off.

The Professor stood and watched him go, taking with him

the collected dreams of a decade. *It can't end like this, it just can't,* he thought as he looked over at the reactor building off in the distance. He then noticed the wreckage of the recent helicopter crash in the foreground, smoke still rising from the smoldering wreckage.

He had a thought. *I wonder if all this has something to do with the occupants of that helicopter?*

31

GHOST IN THE MACHINE

"Sorry, this is going to hurt a bit. Nothing we can really do for broken ribs except bandage them up."

Charles sat on the edge of the gurney, lifted his arms, and let the medic do his job. The cuts on his head had been cleaned and bandaged, and he had a broken left wrist that was now in a cast—he tried not to scratch it. His ribcage hurt like hell, along with most of the rest of his body that still had the ability to feel.

"How's that, too tight?"

"No, fine, fine. Carry on."

"There, I think that's it, all done." The medic stood back and surveyed his handy work. "I'll get you something for the pain."

So far, he'd been shot at, spat at by death drones, almost blown up twice—and his yacht was sunk. He felt a twinge of sadness at its loss. However, he was still alive, and, now that the test was being stopped, it looked like Leonie was out of danger. He would have given a sigh of relief, but it hurt too much.

"Here you go." The medic handed him some painkillers and a glass of water. "Don't take any more than two every four hours."

Charles nodded.

"All patched up?" Madelaine inquired as she returned from her smoke break.

"Yeah, I'm held together with duct tape and staples. So, what now?"

"Debrief. They'll want to get the full story from you. You'll be here for a while."

Charles rubbed his head with his good hand. "Yeah."

"But they're stopping the test, so apocalypse averted," said Madelaine, with a sardonic smile.

"Well, that's good news. And what about you?"

"They're sending a chopper for me, taking me back to *La-La Land*."

Charles laughed. "Stop, don't make me laugh, it hurts too much." He held his side.

"Mr. Gardner?" A tall dapper man with a bowtie stuck his head around the door, he bustled over and offered a hand. "Professor Jason Manderbast. I'm a physicist here at ITER. I need to talk to you, we don't have much time."

Charles shook his hand. "Official debrief?"

The professor looked a little uneasy. "Eh... not quite. The security bigwigs are being somewhat coy with what they know. So this is more of a... private inquiry."

GERALD M. KILBY

"That doesn't sound very encouraging." Charles glanced over at Madelaine. "What's going on?"

"That's a good question. I was rather hoping you could shed some light on that." He then proceeded to give Charles and Madelaine a rundown on what had happened when they tried to shut down the reactor.

"Holy crap, are you serious?" said Madelaine. "I thought they had all this under control?"

"The head of security referred to some intelligence, which he sees fit not to share with any of us physicists. I was wondering if you might know anything about this?"

Charles lifted his good hand, scratched his stubble and contemplated the situation. Leonie was locked in the main ITER control room with God knows how many others, and it seemed that the powers that be had lost control of the reactor or, more likely, someone else was controlling it. Still, he wondered if he should be discussing it with this guy. But then again, could it really make the situation any worse?

"It's a recording," he said finally. "From a surveillance bug. It mentions a plot to sabotage the ITER reactor at the point of ignition—today." He glanced at this watch. "Which gives us less than two hours."

"Do you have it? This recording?" asked Manderbast.

"No, it's on my laptop and that was destroyed in the helicopter crash. I could download it again, but I would need to regenerate the keys to decrypt it. But I don't think we have that much time."

"What can you recall, anything?" the Professor prompted.

198

"I only had time to pick out some keywords like; *autonomous control, lockdown,* something about a *bridge. Cryogenics* was another word they kept mentioning."

"Wait a minute, *cryogenics*?"

"Is that significant?" asked Charles.

"Do you know how a fusion reactor works?"

Charles shook his head. "Only vaguely."

"The core of the reactor here at ITER is a giant metal doughnut, called a Tokamak. It's hollow and contains the reaction fuel, basically a type of hydrogen. This gets heated to 150 million degrees and becomes a plasma. Now, obviously, there is nothing we can build that could withstand that sort of heat, so the plasma is forced into the center of the Tokamak, away from the sides, by a ring of electro-magnets. This stops the reactor from melting. But because these magnets require enormous electrical power, they are made using superconductors, which need to be kept at close to absolute zero, about minus 270 degrees. It's the cryogenic system that performs this function."

"Keep them cold, I see." Charles nodded.

"Yes, but let me explain the problem. There's nearly forty-one billion joules of electrical energy going through these superconductors. If the temperature rises, by even a few degrees, then they lose their superconductivity, and all that energy needs to go somewhere else—find another path."

"Meaning?" said Madelaine.

"Meaning it would be like an Airbus 380 nosediving into the reactor building."

GERALD M. KILBY

"Holy shit!" Madelaine put a hand to her mouth.

"Yes, 'holy shit' indeed. But that's not all. There would also be the problem of radioactivity."

"But I thought fusion reactors weren't radioactive," said Charles.

"Not in the way a nuclear fission reactor is. No, nothing like that. It's not going to be a Chernobyl or Fukushima."

"Well, that's comforting," said Madelaine.

"The radioactivity is tiny by comparison. Instead of lasting a thousand years, it would only be around thirty. But we're still talking about major neutron radiation contamination."

"So let me see if I have this straight," said Madelaine. "We'll know this year's vintage because it's the one glowing in your wine rack."

"Indeed," said Manderbast.

"How are they doing it? That's the question," said Charles. "They said *autonomous control,* so that suggests that something thing outside is controlling it."

"Maybe, but what? They would also need a way in. There's no physical connection between CODAC and the outside world, it's a closed system," said Manderbast.

"CODAC being?" Madelaine asked.

"Control, Data Access, and Communication. It's what runs the test. These processes are just too complex for simple human control. They're all run automatically by CODAC."

Unsurprisingly, Charles's brain began to cycle through several possible ways in which access to CODAC might be achieved. Engineers, by their nature, view life in terms of problems to be solved. Not in the sense that life is just one big problem and no matter how hard you try you will never, ever solve the mystery. No, more like the joy of life is that there are innumerable problems just waiting to be tackled. A world where everything was all figured out would be an engineer's idea of hell. Which leads one to conclude that engineer heaven would contain an infinite number of problems—go figure.

Attention, this is a security announcement. The PA system suddenly blared out an alert. *Will all personnel please proceed to the evacuation rendezvous points.*

"What now?" said Madelaine, as she looked over at the PA speaker.

Several guards then entered the medical center and began to herd people out. "You'll need to come with us, the facility is being evacuated."

"Okay, in a minute," said Madelaine.

"No, we need to go now."

Madelaine flashed her badge. "I said in a minute."

The security guard grumbled and moved on.

"Tell me," Charles turned to the Professor "The people locked in the control room, what happens to them if the reactor goes ker-boom?"

"Some of them might survive. But then there's the radiation."

"Some of them?" Charles's eyebrows arched up to their maximum elevation. "Then we've got to stop it. There has to be a way." He gave the Professor a hard look. "My daughter is in there."

"Oh... I see." Manderbast looked genuinely pained by this news.

Charles began to pace, getting visibly more animated. "How the hell are they doing it? How?"

"I don't know. They've locked us out of our own control systems, so they must be using another one, something powerful, a supercomputer, like MareNostrum. I just don't know."

"MareNostrum? Charles stopped pacing. "I've heard that name before. I think they mentioned it, in the recordings. What is it?"

"It's one of Europe's largest supercomputer. We use it to model all the systems here at ITER," replied the professor.

"But they would still need to make a data connection somehow. Correct?" Charles said this more as a question to himself.

"Yes. The systems here are isolated. No link with the outside world."

Charles suddenly stopped pacing. He had the kernel of an idea. "Where's the ITER data center, the network room?"

A light then seemed to go on in the professor's head. "Yes, yes, I see what you're getting at. MareNostrum knows everything about ITER, right down to the last nut and bolt, literally. If it was hijacked, it could control all the ITER systems. All you need to do is make a physical data connection." His eyes lit up. "A bridge."

"MareNostrum, autonomous control, bridge—it all fits."

Charles felt the pieces clicking into place. "Where's the data center?"

"Not far from the control room, at the far end of the HQ building. There's a covered walkway, a footbridge that leads from this building across to the main ITER site. At the end of the walkway is a tunnel leading into the control room. Just before that, on the right-hand side, is the network room."

"We need to get in there and search it. It's possible they have imbedded a device to circumnavigate the hard firewall. This so-called bridge they mentioned."

"That's close to the reactor, isn't it?" Madelaine gave Charles a concerned look.

He just nodded and shrugged. "What choice do I have?"

Madelaine whipped out her phone. "We need to inform the security chief and get some people in there searching. You don't need to go, Charles."

"They won't know what to look for, or where to look. I do, so I have to go." Charles was empathic and clearly eager not to waste any more time. "Tell them to meet me there. I can give them some direction on what to search for. It will speed things up considerably."

He was about to leave but turned back to Madelaine. "By the way, if I don't see you again, thanks for all your help."

Madelaine rolled her eyes. "There's no need to be so... dramatic. We're not dead yet." She reached out and put a hand on his shoulder, giving him a reassuring squeeze. "Go, before I change my mind and do something stupid like try to be a hero again."

"I'll contact the people at MareNostrum," Manderbast took out his phone. "Get them to stop whatever ITER processes are running. Even if we don't find the *bridge*, then there's still a chance."

Charles nodded. "Okay, good." Then looked over at the exit. "Eh... remind me again, which way is it?"

Manderbast jerked his head toward the door. "Follow me, I'll point you in the right direction." He then turned to Madelaine and nodded. "Very nice to meet you, even if the circumstances are somewhat fraught."

Madelaine already had the phone up to her ear, calling security HQ. "You too," she replied, then gave Charles a last look. "Be careful."

In the background, the PA repeated the evacuation alert. *Attention, this is a security announcement. Will all personnel please proceed to the evacuation rendezvous points.*

32

SMOKE

igh above the Cadarache woodlands, The Patriot slid open the side door of the helicopter and scanned the ITER compound with a pair of binoculars. He spotted the crashed police helicopter, a faint trail of smoke, or possibly steam from the fire hoses, still drifting up from the wreckage. Yet, much to his dismay, he got word that both Gardner and the inspector got out just before it blew up—they were still alive.

Trying to take down the police helicopter in mid-flight had been a big risk. But after Gardner escaped death at the hospital, it was the only option if they were to prevent him reaching ITER. Already, The Patriot knew that a French military chopper was lifting off from an air base, eighty kilometers to the north, and would soon be on patrol over the area, so they had to get out of here, now. He shifted his gaze from the crash site and scanned the hills to the south. He tapped the shoulder of the pilot. "Over there," he shouted. "See that clearing on top of the hill?" The pilot looked and nodded. "Put us down over there." The chopper banked and headed for a clearing about halfway up a wooded hillside.

As the craft made its descent, The Patriot assessed the situation. Charles Gardner was proving to be a tough customer. So far, he had dispatched Mr. Wang and his team along with one of his drones, no mean feat. The drone that the Patriot had on the inspector was also destroyed at the hospital, and all his efforts to stop them reaching ITER had now also failed. He needed to take stock and seek instructions from Xiang Zu, a conversation he was not relishing. The chopper touched down in the clearing and slowed its motors. It couldn't stay here long, not with the threat of military patrols. The Patriot made the call.

Xiang Zu sat in the opulent operations room on board the Helios, sipping white China tea from an ornate porcelain cup. The massive wall screen in front of him still displayed a video feed from the lunar rovers. However, alongside it was also a direct video feed from inside the ITER control room. Elsewhere in the Xiang Zu operation room, technicians monitored data-feeds from both MareNostrum 5 and the ITER CODEC. They were in, they had full control, and Xiang Zu smiled the broadest smile that he had possibly ever achieved in his entire life. That was until The Patriot's head popped up on a conference feed and began talking.

Xiang Zu considered this new information from his trusted drone tech. As it stood, everything else was going according to plan, and ITER would soon be a big ball of radiated vapor. Even if Gardner was still alive and on the loose, there was nothing he or anyone else could do now to stop the inevitable destruction of the reactor.

Nevertheless, he had lost Mr. Wang and some good men in the quest to destroy the evidence of the French agent's assassination, and Gardner was still in possession of a potentially incriminating recording. In reality though, Xiang Zu was not overly concerned about that. However, what did concern him was the fact that Gardner was becoming a real pain in the ass. Therefore, he had to die, along with that meddling Monaco Police Inspector.

"I need them dead as soon as possible. We can't have any loose ends," said Xiang Zu. "This is now in your hands, so what do you plan to do about it?"

Fortunately for The Patriot, this was the very question he wanted to hear. "We'll send the helicopter back to our logistics hub in Marseille, fly low over Lake Sainte-Croix, and dump all the weapons. That way if it's intercepted there's no evidence on board—just out for a spot of sightseeing. Myself and one other will stay here and set up camp. Then I'll release the hunter seeker drone swarm—and take Gardner and the inspector out, once and for all."

"Good," said Xiang Zu. "Very good. Make it so."

The Patriot nodded and signed off. Xiang Zu took another sip of tea. He had stopped smiling. In fact, he decided he would exercise more stringent self-control until the final objective was reached. No more frivolity—the shore was now in sight.

The wash from the departing helicopter buffeted The Patriot as he carried a bulky aluminum flight case further up the hill and under the cover of some trees. Behind him was Efraim Raker, a fellow countryman, an Israeli and a competent drone operator. He too labored up the hill with two smaller cases. When they reached cover, they set down the cases, opened them, and began to prepare the *swarm*.

The Patriot popped the lid on the larger case. Inside, nestled in contoured foam, were nine insect drones similar in size and weaponry to the others he had lost. However, by using state of the art control software, these all operated as a swarm. Only one needed to be controlled and the others would follow in unison, keeping pace with the lead drone and tracking their position relative to one another. They could compensate for most obstacles in their path and always try to realign themselves with the swarm formation. To see them in flight, hunting, seeking, was to witness an aerial ballet of consummate beauty.

They activated each of the drones and then flipped open the two control cases, one primary and one backup. They checked, tested, and finally they let them fly. The Patriot watched as the swarm rose up above the treetops and tracked over toward the ITER compound.

He reckoned that Gardner and the inspector were most likely in or around the medical center since that would be the logical place for two injured people to be brought to. He reckoned correctly because it was not long before he got a visual on the inspector—out having a cigarette. The Patriot grinned. "Did nobody ever tell you, Inspector, that smoking is very bad for your health?"

33

DON'T DO ANYTHING STUPID

M adelaine stood outside the entrance to the medical center. Excited groups of people were already assembling, milling around in animated conversation. Many were on their phones—word was getting out.

"Please remain calm, it's just a precautionary measure, nothing to be concerned about." One of the security guards was placating an agitated group. "Transport will be here shortly to take you to a rendezvous point outside the facility."

"What's going on?" asked a young anxious woman.

"Nothing to worry about. Just a security precaution."

Madelaine wandered off to the side of the group, sat down on the edge of a flower box, and took out a flattened packet of cigarettes. "You can't smoke here," said a surly guard.

Madelaine flashed her badge at him. "So shoot me." She

extracted a usable smoke out of the packet, lit it from a book of matches stuffed in the wrapper, and took a deep drag. The guard wisely decided to ignore her.

She had just come off the phone to Jean-Luc Bastion and had given him a run down on how the reactor was being compromised as best she could. He assured her that they would send a team over to the network room and investigate. However, now that she was off the phone and had some time to think, she got a sense that Bastion might have been simply placating her. He did say investigate, not assist. Then again, maybe she was just being paranoid.

Yet what more could she realistically do? Taking off with Charles and the Professor would serve no good purpose, she would be of little use. This was a job for tech-nerds, not gun-slingers. She would just be taking a foolish risk with her life and she didn't want to make Leon an orphan—just yet.

Madelaine looked down along the length of the massive HQ building. At the far end, she could see the covered bridge crossing over the road into the main ITER site. She wondered if they had made it that far. She then cast her gaze across to the gigantic reactor building off in the distance. *A sun in a box,* she thought. *God's power station.* She rolled the cigarette filter between her thumb and finger and flicked across the tarmac, then shook another one out of the packet. The guard gave her a grim look.

"So shoot me again." But she didn't light it, instead she slid her phone out of her pocket and thumbed up the chief's number in the Monaco Harbor Police Department and hit dial. He answered almost immediately.

"Madelaine!"

"Hello, Régis"

"The Prince is going to be very pissed off with you."

"Screw the Prince—never liked him anyway."

"Yeah well, you can take your place at the back of the queue on that one. So, what the hell happened?"

"Someone tried to take me out."

"I'm assuming you don't mean romantically."

"Remind me again how you got to be Chief of Police."

"What were you thinking, Madelaine, heading off to Cadarache? You were supposed to just interview him, not take him on a sightseeing tour of Provence."

"It seemed like the right thing to do at the time."

"You could have got yourself killed. It was a crazy thing to do."

"Yes, well, hindsight is always 20/20."

There was a pause on the line before Régis spoke again. "Anyway, are you okay?"

"Yeah, I'm still operational."

"Any ideas who was taking pot shots at you?"

"If I were to guess, I'd say it was Xiang Zu's people."

"And that Gardner guy, how is he?"

"He's pretty shook up, not used to people trying to kill him all day long."

Another momentary pause as Régis collected his thoughts "This... recording of his, have you heard it?"

"No, I think Inspector LeMon had a copy when he got nailed by that drone in the hospital in Nice. I don't know what happened to it."

"So nobody's heard this except Gardner. How do we know it actually exists, that it's not some figment of his imagination? I mean think about it, Madelaine. First, he starts with this murdered woman story, then when he gets no traction with that, it ratchets up a load of notches into a terrorist plot. Have you ever considered that this may all be in his mind?"

"Sure, it's a possibility, but I don't think so. Fifteen minutes ago, the control room at reactor facility here went into lockdown—all by itself. Nothing gets in, nothing gets out, and they don't seem to be in control of it. So, something's going down, and, if Gardner is right, then in a little over an hour, the facility goes boom and everybody in the control room gets vaporized. And another thing, Gardner's daughter is in there, one of the news team."

"Oh."

"Yeah, so, you know what? I hope you're right, Régis. I hope it's all in his head."

"Okay, okay. Just saying, that's all. Anyway, we're sending a chopper for you now, so hang in there and don't do anything stupid. You hear?"

"I'll do my best. Bye." Madelaine put the phone back in her pocket and lit the cigarette. She watched the smoke as it trailed skyward in the warm, still air. Then something caught her eye. Way off in the distance, she spotted a helicopter shaped dot. She squinted to try and better make it out.

"Any idea who that helicopter belongs to?" She pointed it out to the guard, who was still beside her.

He shaded his eyes with a hand. "Nope, could be anyone. But it's probably just a news channel."

Madelaine tracked its movement as landed down on a distant hill for a brief moment before it rose again and headed south toward the coast. She watched it disappear, and thought no more about it.

A short time later, Madelaine heard the bus that was to take them to the evacuation point trundle along the front of the HQ building. She would have to take it, since the chopper that Régis was sending would not be allowed to land inside the ITER compound. The crowd had quieted down now, all were looking in the direction of the advancing transport.

Then she heard it, a soft buzzing high overhead. The sound of a large insect, or possibly several large insects.

Zizz... zizz...

She stood upright and strained her ears, listening for the sound again, but it was gone. The noise of the approaching bus began to drown out all other sounds. It stopped in front of them with rumble and a wheeze of brakes, and the assembled crowd began to climb on board.

"Come on." The guard gestured toward the transport.

She nodded, stubbed out her cigarette, and headed over to get on the bus.

34

A BRIDGE TO A BRIDGE

"Yes, yes... keep trying, you have to keep trying." Professor Jason Manderbast shoved his phone back into his pocket as the elevator door closed. "They can't get through to the institute where MareNostrum is." He hit the button for the second floor of the HQ building. "They're sending a team over there, but you have to realize this is over in Barcelona, Spain. It's a different country, different jurisdiction, and it's also a religious holiday there today. I'm not sure they're going to be in time."

"Could I use your phone?" Charles asked as they stepped out of the elevator.

"Sure." The professor took it out of his pocket and handed it to him.

"Thanks. I want to try and contact Leonie."

The professor shook his head. "There's no point. There's no phone communication within the control room. It's a security measure in case phones are used to trigger a device."

Charles tried anyway.

"The walkway entrance is just down here, come on." Manderbast raced ahead, down the corridor.

Charles had the phone to his ear. *Sorry but the person you are calling...*

"Dammit." He shoved the phone into his pocket and started after the professor.

Then he heard a sound that sent a shiver down his spine.

Zizz... zizz...

He ducked into a doorway alcove, pressed his back to the wall and kept still, listening intently. He could hear the drone at the far end of the corridor. He pulled the phone back out of his pocket, switched on the forward-facing camera, and held it like a mirror so he could see down the corridor. He spotted the drone moving slowly toward him, still on the far side of the walkway entrance. But the professor was nowhere to be seen. He pulled the phone back in.

Dammit, he thought. *What to do, what to do?*

The buzzing grew fainter, so he checked corridor again, this time the drone was nowhere to be seen. *Where the hell is it?* He listened intently but couldn't hear it. If it went down along the walkway, then the professor was in real danger. Manderbast would have no idea what it was, nor its deadly payload.

Charles calmed himself and continued listening for the telltale buzzing sound to return, but it didn't. It had either moved off out of earshot or had stopped completely. He checked the corridor again with the phone camera but still couldn't spot it—he wasn't sure if this was a good thing or a bad thing. But time was running out, he'd have to get moving again. Charles steeled himself and stuck his head out from the doorway. There was no sign of the drone.

He took a step out, glanced up and down the corridor, and headed off toward the walkway entrance. He had only gone a few steps when it struck—swooping down from the ceiling. Charles stumbled backward, tripped, and ended up on his ass as the drone hovered above him—getting ready to strike.

Phitt... phitt... Two darts spat out from its underbelly.

Charles instinctively jerked his arm up to protect his face, and, lucky for him, the darts buried themselves harmlessly in his recently acquired plaster cast. The drone danced in the air and tried to find a better angle of attack. Charles was now scrambling backward on all fours, trying to keep the drone in sight, and his arm elevated. But he knew he couldn't keep evading it like this. Any moment now, this drone was going to end his life.

Then it exploded.

Madelaine strode into view around the doorway, gun in hand. She stood over the buzzing remains of the drone as it spun in dizzying circles on the ground, and stamped on it, twisting her heel as she did.

"Die...bitch." She turned to where Charles had collapsed on the floor. "You okay?"

Charles had felt the impact of numerous metallic shards on

the side of his face when the drone disintegrated. He brought his hand up, delicately feeling around for any of the deadly barbs, and breathed a sigh of relief when he found none.

Madelaine reached out and offered a hand to help him up.

"You sure know how to make an entrance." He grabbed her outstretched hand and pulled himself vertical. As he stood, he felt a little unsteady and hung onto Madelaine for support. They came together and embraced. His body shook as he clutched her tight to him. "Thanks... for coming back. You saved my life."

"I heard the drones outside. I had to warn you."

"Sorry, I've caused you nothing but trouble since we met."

She tightened her embrace. "It's okay. I've a knack for finding it anyway, or maybe it finds me." They pulled apart and looked at one another.

"We need to go," said Madelaine.

Charles nodded.

"Where's the professor?" she asked, looking around.

"I don't know, he ran ahead of me. He could have reached the network room."

"Assuming the drone didn't get him first," cautioned Madelaine.

"True." Charles hung his head. "We'd better go and find out." He turned, walked to the edge of the doorway alcove, and tentatively peered around the corner. The corridor was empty as far as he could see, so they made their way quietly along it, keeping tight to the wall until they got to the entrance for the walkway overpass.

This was a long, glass-sided footbridge that led directly into a tunnel on the far side, which terminated at the entrance to the Tokamak control room. This would be sealed off during lockdown, and there was no way in or out. But somewhere along the tunnel was a door that should lead into the network room. They kept very quiet as they moved, all the time listening for any telltale sound of a drone. They heard none.

Madelaine peered around the corner and down along the length of the walkway overpass. She held her pistol high, ready to shoot if any drone popped up.

"Damn."

"What is it?" asked Charles as he stood with his back to the corridor wall.

"I think it's Professor Manderbast."

Charles tentatively looked down the length of the walkway. Sunlight flooded through its glass sides, the structural beams casting a multitude of confused geometric shapes across the floor. The tunnel entrance at the far end was in darkness, punctuated only by the strobe of an amber flashing light. Slumped on the floor, just at the entrance, he could make out the motionless form of Professor Jason Manderbast.

"Professor?" Charles ventured a call. The body remained motionless.

"He's not moving," said Madelaine.

"Jason?" he ventured again, but there was no sign of life. "I think he's either paralyzed or dead."

Madelaine took a peek. "Looks like that drone must have nailed him."

"He could be still alive," said Charles. "If he is, we need to get him on a ventilator, that would save him. I'm pretty sure it's curare that's used in those darts. It paralyzes all the muscles except the heart—you die by asphyxiation. A ventilator would keep him alive until the effects wear off. I saw some back at the medical center when I was getting bandaged up." Charles glanced at his watch. "Fifty-nine minutes to ignition, we'd better hurry."

Madelaine stepped cautiously along the side wall of the walkway. Charles followed. He could feel his heart beating in his chest, his hands were sweating, and every fiber in his body was tuned for flight at the slightest trigger.

Zizz... zizz...

Another drone burst out from the darkness of the tunnel. Madelaine fired off two shots, the drone dodged, and moved back into concealment. They both then turned and ran back along the walkway, toward a small, open dining area just ahead of them.

"This way," Charles pointed, as they ran past the dining tables, and through a set of heavy swing doors into the kitchen area.

"Dammit, there's no way out, we're trapped," said Madelaine as she looked around for another door.

They both cautiously went back to the swing doors, which were designed for catering staff moving in and out of the kitchen and had small round windows fitted at head height. They peered back out at the kitchen area, looking for the drone.

They could see across the open dining area, out past the corridor, and directly along the length of the walkway.

Charles listened intently. He could hear to the ambient sounds of the facility. An aural tapestry began to unfold as he focused on processing sound. The base canvas was a background hum of fluorescent lights over which was laid the rhythm of kitchen appliances, fridges and freezers, kicking in and out. Finally, he heard it.

Zizz... zizz...

Though the window, he could see the small drone flying into the dining area, then another, and another—they kept on coming. The drones began forming themselves into an evenly spaced matrix, each one equidistant from the next—eight in total. From the shape of the matrix, it looked like there should be nine. Perhaps that was the one Madelaine destroyed earlier. The drones hovered in the center of the dining area for a minute then they all split apart, darting this way and that, hunting, sensing, seeking.

"Goddammit, we'll never make it through all of those," said Madelaine, shaking her head.

One finally spotted them and darted over to the kitchen doors, analyzing them through the windows with its dual cameras. Charles raised his middle finger and mouthed *go screw yourself.* Madelaine raised her pistol to shoot.

"No, wait." Charles raised a hand. "You might get that one, but the others would be on top of us."

Madelaine lowered the weapon. "Dammit. So how the hell do we get out of here?" She unclipped the magazine out of the

SIG-Sauer handgun and checked the rounds. "Only five left." She snapped it back in and looked around the kitchen. "Maybe we could use something as a shield. I don't think those darts have much penetration, might give us a fighting chance."

"Wait," said Charles, "I've an idea. See if you can find me a large plastic mixing bowl and a roll of tinfoil."

Madelaine gave him an incredulous look. "Now is not the time to be mixing up some cookie dough."

But Charles was already wrestling an industrial sized microwave from its shelf in the kitchen. "And a sharp serrated knife," he called back over his shoulder.

Madelaine gave a sigh, holstered her weapon, and came over to him. "Here, let me help you with that."

He smiled at her. "Thanks, my body aches all over."

"Any chance you could tell me what you are up to here?" Madelaine asked as they lifted the heavy appliance over to a counter.

"It's hard to explain." He reached into his pocket and pulled out a multi-tool. "Give me a minute or two and you'll see."

Madelaine looked at her watch. "Forty-eight minutes to ignition test. Whatever it is you're doing, you'll need to hurry."

Charles began removing the metal case from the microwave, exposing its innards, as Madelaine began rooting through cupboards and drawers. "Plastic, not metal?"

"Yeah, plastic... and tinfoil. Lots of tinfoil."

"I hope you're not planning on making a tinfoil hat to communicate with the aliens." She held up a large mixing bowl. "Will this do?"

"Perfect," said Charles.

She put it on the counter along with a roll of catering tinfoil and some knives. "What is that thing?" Madelaine was looking at a large component Charles had just removed from the disemboweled appliance—a heavy metal box, with a pointy bit on one side.

"This is called a *Magnetron*. It's the business end of a microwave."

"You're going to microwave the drones?"

Charles looked at her with sly smile. "That's the plan." He began cutting a hole in the bottom of the mixing bowl, then covered the inside with tinfoil. "See if you can find some sticky tape or string." He went over to rip out a long length of electrical cable that was being used for a TV. It took Charles another few valuable minutes to finish the machine. The tinfoil cone was now attached to the magnetron, and it had the look of a 1950's B-movie ray-gun.

"Will it work?" said Madelaine a little skeptically.

"Let's do a test." He unscrewed a fluorescent tube from one of the light fittings and placed it on the ground at the far end of the kitchen. He lifted the magnetron, pointed it at the tube, and flicked the switch. The tube glowed with an intense brightness.

"Wow, that's the most amazing thing I've seen in a long time. How does it work? Actually, forget that, I really don't need to know, and we don't have the time."

Charles swung the machine around to face the doors. "Okay, let's go and fry some drones."

Madelaine took out her pistol, moved over beside the swing

doors, and peered out. The drones had taken up resting positions sitting on various tables in the main dining area, waiting, conserving energy, all the while keeping Charles and Madelaine pinned down in the kitchen. Charles tapped on the glass and the drones reacted immediately, they twitched and flexed their wings and rose up in the air in unison, forming a hovering grid pattern.

"All right, here goes." He aimed the magnetron at the center of the drone swarm and flicked the switch. Four of them dropped straight out of the air and hit the floor. Another did a kind of backwards flip and then it too crashed to the ground. The other three scattered out of sight.

"It worked. You did it," said Madelaine.

Charles scanned the dining room floor. Four drones were down and inert, and one buzzed and twitched and spun around on the floor in dizzying circles. "There's three still operational out there," he said, then looked at his watch. "Twenty-five minutes to ignition, we'd better hurry. Do you see any of the others?"

"Look. Over there, by the window." Two drones rose off the floor where they had been squatting and moved slowly toward them, then halted, hovering in position.

"They're keeping their distance."

"Yeah, whoever's controlling them saw the others go down so they're taking no chances," said Charles.

"Can you get them at that range?"

"Unlikely, I'll need to get closer." He shouldered the door open just a crack. The drones reacted instantly, darting forward.

Phhit... phhit...

Two needles embedded themselves in the edge of the door as Charles backed off just in time. But the drones were now considerably closer, so he quickly lifted the magnetron and flicked the switch—the drones dropped out of the air.

"Wow, I'm never going to think of a microwave the same way ever again," said Madelaine.

Charles looked at his watch. "Twenty minutes until the test starts."

"And the whole place goes boom," Madelaine replied.

"There's still one more of those bastards out there," Charles scanned the dining area. "See anything?"

"Nope. But I think we should just go for it."

"You're right, we're running out of time."

Madelaine leveled her pistol, gripping it with both hands. "Ready?" she looked over at Charles.

He lowered his makeshift ray gun onto the floor. "Pity we can't take this with us."

Madelaine shouldered the swing door open, and they crept out into the dining area, stepping around dead drones. She scanned the room, flicking her gun this way and that.

"I don't see it," she whispered. "Let's keep moving."

They entered the corridor and started down the long walkway toward the prostrate form of Professor Jason Manderbast. Through the glass sides of the overpass, they could see across the ITER campus. It was completely deserted, save for themselves and the people trapped in the control room. They crept silently along, senses on high alert. Madelaine reached down and checked the slumped figure of the Professor for a pulse. "Dead."

Across his forehead, five needles were embedded in his flesh.

"He didn't have a chance, did he?" said Charles.

They moved forward into the control room entrance tunnel, the amber flashing lights illuminating their way. In the background, they could hear a security announcement echoing from somewhere up ahead.

Attention, ignition test in T minus eight minutes.

"This is it." Charles halted at a door marked *Network Room* and tried the handle. "Locked."

"Stand back." Madelaine fired a shot and the lock disintegrated. She kicked it open, revealing stairs descending to a deeper level. They headed down, lights flickering on as they moved. The air was much cooler here, and the side walls were cold to the touch. At the bottom of the stairs, a vast room opened out with aisles and aisles of cabinets full of computer servers. It was also filled with the sound of a thousand cooling fans busy keeping the servers at optimal temperature. A strobing amber light flashed, and above the noise of the cooling fans they could hear, *Attention, ignition test in T minus five minutes.*

"What exactly are we looking for?" said Madelaine as she scanned the racks of servers.

"According to the Professor, there should be a comms room at the far end. We'll need to find it fast."

They ran through the rows of servers until Charles finally

halted and pointing to a small glass walled room. "There, that must be it."

It was locked. Madelaine fired another shot at the door, and it shattered into a thousand pieces. Charles stepped in and looked around. *Attention, ignition test in T minus three minutes.*

Charles examined the equipment. Several racks of comms gear stood either side of a large industrial-looking switch panel with two key slots and a digital readout—which was currently reading *offline*. Charles drew closer to one of the racks. "This is it, this is where all the fiber optic cables come in from the outside. They're connected to CODAC via this switch box. They must have bridged it, bypassing it somehow."

Attention, ignition test in T minus two minutes.

Charles began tracing cables coming into the switch panel.

The flashing strobe lights suddenly changed from amber to red.

"Dammit, we're too late," said Madelaine.

Warning, negative fluctuation in cryogenic systems.

Then Charles spotted something very odd. Clamped around one of the incoming fiber optic cables was what looked like a traditional wristwatch.

Warning, critical temperature deviation in cryogenic systems.

"I think I found it." He pulled out his multi-tool and snipped the ties attaching the watch device to the cable. He held it in his hand and examined it. "A wireless bridge, clever," he said, as he set about finding and disconnecting the other half of the watch device.

The strobing warning lights turned amber, then stopped. Charles and Madelaine looked at each other.

"You did it, you actually did it." Madelaine threw her arms around him and squeezed him tight."

"Ahhhh... not so tight. My ribs are killing me."

"Oops, sorry."

Then they heard it.

Zizz... zizz...

Madelaine spun around and reached for her gun.

Phitt... phitt... phitt...

She fired off two shots, and the drone disintegrated.

"Oh shit." She pulled two of the deadly darts out from her neck, and looked over at Charles, who was pulling a dart from the back of his hand.

"Ventilator, now, quick! Charles shouted. "Let's go before it begins to take effect."

They ran back through the computer racks and started up the stairs when Madelaine started to slow down.

"Ohhhh, I'm beginning to feel it." She leaned her back against the side wall.

Charles pulled her arm around his shoulder and helped her move again. "Keep going, you've got to keep going."

They struggled up the stairs. Charles could feel Madelaine's strength failing. By the time they got to the footbridge, she was having difficulty putting one foot in front of the other. "You've got to keep going, you can't give up."

"I... can't. Can't... move. Sorry."

It was no use, she wasn't going to make it to the medical

center where the ventilators were, and Charles was starting to feel the effects himself—he was slowing, getting weaker. He laid her down on the floor and hurried off to the canteen area. A half minute later, he ran back, this time with a stainless steel catering trolley on wheels. He lifted her up onto it as best he could and started pushing her along in front of him toward the elevator.

By the time he got her inside, her breathing had become labored as the effects of the curare slowly paralyzed her muscles. "Hang in there Madelaine, just hang in there."

The elevator door opened, and he pushed the trolley out, but he was losing strength. It felt like he was pushing a car up hill. He forced his body to respond and managed to get some momentum going. Down the long corridor to the medical center, he pushed and pushed, with each step he could feel the strength sapping from him. He looked down at Madelaine, she was still breathing, but very shallow. He only had minutes to get her onto the ventilator or she would be dead. He pushed through the doors of the deserted clinic and over to where he had seen the machines earlier. He lost his footing and fell on the floor. His body was succumbing to the toxin. "Move, goddammit, move." He forced himself to crawl over to the machine and pull himself upright. His eyes were losing focus as he tried to figure it out. It was much more complicated than he had imagined. It was a mess of tubes and wires. He tried to focus, but he was losing control of his limbs. He slumped to the floor and realized it was game over.

I just can't do it. I can't save her, he thought as he used the last of his strength to look over at the stricken form of Inspector Madelaine Duchamp. He had no more to give. He fell sideways across the floor and began losing consciousness, entering the twilight zone.

Somewhere in the distance, he thought he heard footsteps, then voices talking to him—then nothing at all.

35

A DIFFERENT TIME

Marcel's last memory was of the ground rushing toward him after he had been flung off his motorbike when it slammed into the roadside barrier. Consciousness now returned to him in waves of ever more lucid dreams that steadily grew in clarity. And with this clarity came questions. *What's that sound? What's that light?* Consciousness finally came to Marcel with the question, *where the hell am I?*

He was in Nice General Hospital and had been there for several weeks. They had put him into an induced coma to aid his body and repair the brain damage caused by the crash. He had broken the radius of the left arm, his left collarbone, several ribs, and most of the rest of his body was one big purple bruise. But the danger to his life came from head injuries. Marcel's skull was intact, but his brain had swelled and stubbornly refused all initial efforts by the medical team to recede. Now, though, they felt it safe to bring him back and assess his level of functioning.

After a seemingly endless battery of cognitive tests, it was concluded that he did indeed see the correct number of fingers held up in front of him, and that he would live to fight another day. He had come through the entire ordeal surprisingly unscathed, all things considered. Another three weeks were spent regaining his strength with physiotherapy sessions and light exercise in the hospital pool.

During his time recuperating, he watched news channels and read—a lot. He felt that the crash had rewired his brain in some bizarre way, because now he had a voracious appetite for information. He read everything he could get his hands on— books, magazines, news sites. It was like he was seeing the world for the very first time.

He read about the successful ignition test of the ITER reactor—it was hard not to, it was front page news everywhere. An endless array of pundits and scientific commentators waxed lyrically about the implications for human civilization. Yet, Marcel's fascination was not merely academic. What interested him most was the side story, the rumors of an attempt by foreign agents to sabotage the reactor. The story was always followed by dramatic footage of a French naval vessel boarding the Helios as it made passage for the Suez Canal. Xiang Zu was not on board.

This explained a lot to Marcel. It explained why he had not been contacted by anyone in the Xiang Zu hierarchy since regaining consciousness, and probably why he was still alive and hadn't yet been assassinated. But he also knew that it would only be a matter of time before he himself became a person of interest to the authorities. And so it was, six weeks after the crash, that he had his one and only visitor.

Sunlight streamed through the blinds and radiated shadows across the floor of Marcel's hospital room. He sat in a stiff, high-backed armchair, sipping on a bottle of water and reading a book. He was also having a serious cigarette craving, the first in a few days. He hadn't smoked since the day of the crash. The door opened to his room and Marcel assumed it must be time for another physiotherapy session. He put down the book and stood up. To his surprise, Sofia du Maurier, one of the hospitality crew of the *Helios*, entered the room.

"Hello, Marcel. How are you feeling?"

"Sofia?" He gave her a curious look, not sure of what to make of this encounter. He didn't know her that well, and certainly not well enough for her to risk coming to visit him.

"Not what you were expecting?"

"Eh... no, I mean... considering all that happened."

"Yes, well I can understand I'm probably the last person you would expect a visit from, but there's a lot you don't know about me, Marcel." She came over to one of the armchairs opposite him and sat down. Marcel eyes followed her, a perplexed expression on his face.

"So, how are you feeling?" she asked.

"They say I'll live."

"That's good, it was quite a nasty crash you had. You're lucky to be alive."

"In more ways than one, I imagine."

Sofia considered him for a moment. "I'm here to find out what happened to Marika."

Marcel looked at her. "Is that why you came, to ask about Marika?" He leaned back in the chair. "Tell you what, let's start by you telling me who you really are. Because something tells me you are not simply a lowly cabin girl, are you?"

"Okay." She adjusted herself in the chair, then looked directly at him. "The truth is, I'm a French Intelligence Agent. I was on board the Helios to find out what Xiang Zu was up to. We suspected he was stealing industrial data and using the Helios as the operations center. I was embedded as part of the crew to find out how it was being done."

Marcel stared at her as the implications of her confession began to sink in. "So... what you're saying is... Marika wasn't a spy?"

Sofia shook her head. "No."

Marcel put his head in his hands and looked at the floor. Then his hand then went to the cross around his neck. *She wasn't an agent,* he thought. *She wasn't playing me.*

Sofia leaned toward him. She lowered her voice "We know she was murdered, Marcel. We're hoping you can tell us how, and who did it?"

Marcel stared at the floor for some time, shaking his head and fingering the cross with one hand. Eventually he stood up, walked over to the window, and looked out across the hospital campus.

"I think it's my turn to tell you something about me that you don't know." He talked with his back to her. "There was a time, not so long ago, when I would have cut your throat just as easy as talk. But that was a different time and a different me. I've changed since then." He turned around. "It was Marika that started that change in me. Not that she knew it, it was subtle at first. But she opened doors that made me question the world, question myself." He returned to armchair and sat in silent thought.

"What happened to her, Marcel?"

"What happened?" He gave her a long cold look. "They thought she was you, an agent." He leaned back in the chair and sighed. "Mr. Wang called me one evening, said he wanted help cleaning up some shit, asked me to meet him down at the stern bay diving platform on board the Helios. It was only when I got there that I realized what was going on. Marika was tied up and in a mess, bloodied, battered—presumably they tried to beat a confession out of her." Marcel lowered his face and turned back to face Sofia. "She had that look, the look a person has when they know they are going to die. Then, before I had time to think, Xiang Zu put a bullet in her head." He fingered the cross again.

"So Xiang Zu pulled the trigger?" asked Sofia.

"Yes. He pulled the trigger." Marcel sat down again gave her a critical look. "You're not much of an agent, are you? You got a civilian killed, you didn't know about the plot to sabotage ITER, and in the end you lost your man. I heard he wasn't on the Helios when you seized it."

"We'll find him."

"Ha, ha, no you won't. Not if he doesn't want to be found."

Sofia said nothing for a moment. "I'm sorry about Marika, I really am. We had become friends. And yes, maybe I got her killed. But I didn't pull the trigger, Marcel."

Marcel leaned forward and, almost in a whisper, said, "I know where he is. Xiang Zu, I know where to find him."

"Where? You need to tell us."

He sat back again. "Well, that would all depend on what you plan to do to him."

36

ONE IS ALL IT TAKES

A hot dry sun beat down on the busy market square in the port city of Algiers. A sea of people thronged the stalls, moving and shifting, haggling and hustling, securing their provisions for the day. Marcel scanned the throng as they swirled with the ebb and flow of the market. From his rooftop vantage point, he had a wide sweeping view all across the market below.

He crouched down, unclipped the catches on the slim flight case, and opened the lid to reveal a precision sniper rifle. Slowly and methodically, he assembled the weapon. He put one round in the chamber. *One is all it takes,* he considered. He then kicked out the short stand and poked the muzzle of the rifle through a gap in the rooftop wall. He looked through the scope and scanned the market throng again. Once he was satisfied that everything was in order, he set the butt of the gun back down and used his binoculars to survey the crowd. Taking a sip of water from a bottle, he settled himself in for a long wait.

When the plot to ITER had been exposed, a French frigate was dispatched to intercept the Helios before it made it through the Suez Canal. The boat was seized, and all passengers and crew held for interview, but there was no sign of Xiang Zu, nor Lao Bang. They had both escaped using a small submersible that was housed in the bowels of the super yacht. It slipped passed the French navy presence and out into the Mediterranean. It was hours before they even knew he had escaped. However, it only had a limited range, so it had to have berthed somewhere along the North African coast. Marcel had spent the best part of a decade with Xiang Zu and knew a considerable amount about his operations in Algeria and Libya. If Xiang Zu wanted to lie low for a while in this part of the world, then Marcel knew exactly where that would be.

After Sofia had left him in the hospital, he was interviewed several more times over the next two weeks by various agents. But they had nothing on him—he knew that, and so did they. When it seemed that they were about to give up trying, he approached Sofia and cut a deal. He reckoned, correctly, she would jump at the opportunity to save something from her disastrous mission on board the Helios and get herself back in the good books with the agency. In the end, all parties considered it a win-win. They would all get closure, so to speak. And so it was that he found himself back where he had first met Xiang Zu all those years ago when he was just a boy.

The sun was still early in the sky as Marcel wiped a bead of sweat from his forehead. He had been keeping watch for some time now and his shoulder began to ache—he was not fully healed yet from the accident, and probably never would be. Then he saw him, walking through the busy throng like a prince. Marcel put down the binoculars and shouldered the rifle. He scanned the market again with the scope and finally spotted him in the crosshairs. He calmed his breathing and steadied the rifle. Xiang Zu stopped at the stall of a date seller —the merchant offered him some dates, a tasty treat to tempt a customer. Xiang Zu smacked his lips, gesticulating with an appreciative wave of his hand to his entourage.

Then the right side of his head exploded.

Marcel watched through the scope as Xiang Zu fell to the ground, the crowd around him diving for cover. "For Marika," he whispered. He quickly disassembled the weapon, being careful not to expose his body above the low parapet wall. They would be looking to find where the shot came from, and he didn't want to give his position away. Once it was packed up in the flight case, he walked over to the stairs and descended in a quick skipping rhythm. At the bottom, he carefully opened the door to the back street and walked a few short steps to his waiting car. He put the case in the trunk, locked it, and got into the driver's seat. He drove to the end of the side street and turned in to the early morning traffic. Through the open window, he could hear the sound of sirens, all heading for the market.

He drove south out of the city and after a while the traffic thinned as he turned onto the A1 heading southwest across the fertile Mitidja Plain. Twenty minutes later, he reached Chiffa and turned due south to take him through the Atlas Mountains. It was not long before the road started to twist and turn as the landscape around him grew higher and higher. Soon he came to the point where he had been instructed to turn off. This was an old dirt road that wound its way into the heart of the mountains. After a further twenty minutes of driving, it finally ended at an old abandoned house. He knew he was at the right place as there was a big black 4x4 parked up ahead. He drove up beside it, stopped, and got out. He walked over to the 4x4, opened the back door, and got in. Sitting in the back seat was Sofia du Maurier.

He handed his keys to her. "You'll find the rifle in the trunk."

She took the keys and passed them to her driver, a young man with a naïve eager expression. He accepted them and got out to retrieve the weapon, like a faithful hound. Sofia picked up a thick manila envelope from the seat and handed it to Marcel. "As agreed."

He opened it and looked inside. It contained several thick bundles of five-hundred euro notes. He placed it back down on the seat between them without counting. "I want you to do something for me."

"That would depend." Sofia gave him a curious look.

From his pocket Marcel withdrew an old tattered letter. He handed it to Sofia. "I want you to send the money to the address on the letter. It's Marika's family."

She nodded. "I'm sure we could do that for you. But how are we going to explain where it came from?"

Marcel gave a short laugh. "Well, you are French Intelligence, so just use some of that *intelligence* and figure it out."

Sofia slid the letter into the envelope with the money. "Okay, I'm sure we can dream up with something vaguely plausible."

"Thanks." He made a move to leave the confines of the car when Sofia stopped him.

"Before you go." She handed him a small business card—blank except for one phone number.

Marcel examined it, flipping it over in his hands. "So what's this?"

"If you ever think of working for the good guys, just call that number. You'd be a good man to have in a fight, assuming we're on the same side."

Marcel laughed and handed the card back to her. "I made that mistake once before. I'm done with that now."

"Keep it, you might need it someday," said Sofia.

Marcel put it in his pocket. "If it makes you happy, but I don't think so." He opened the car door and got out. Sofia called after him "So where to now?"

He turned back to her and then his gaze looked to the west across the mountains. "To where violence is only a memory." He waved goodbye and walked over to his car.

37

LIGHTHOUSE

Early morning sun bathed the old venetian port of Chania on the island of Crete, bringing with it the promise of a bright new day. The ancient stone lighthouse at the harbor mouth cast a long shadow over the moored boats, marking out time like an imperious sun dial, doing so today as it has done for over five hundred years. Where once its shadow fell on the merchant fleets of ancient Mediterranean city states, now it simply watched over a few small fishing boats and a scattering of holiday yachts.

Madelaine Duchamp sat in the salon of one such yacht, reading an old book she had found in the market the previous day. It was called *The Count of Montecristo*, about a man who escaped the seeming impossible. On her lap, a small dog snuggled into her.

When Charles disconnected the comms bridge in the ITER

network room, the lockdown ceased, and the doors to the control room finally opened. A team of medical staff was immediately dispatched to assess the needs of those who had had the misfortune to be trapped in there. While en route, the team swung by the medical center to make preparations, only to find two bodies slumped beside a ventilator unit in ICU. On closer examination they were both found to be still alive, but only barely. Fortunately, quick work by the medical team and the fact that they were already in ICU meant that they were quickly stabilized. A few hours later, both regained consciousness and soon after could breathe unaided.

For Madelaine's part in thwarting the potential catastrophic destruction of the ITER reactor and subsequent loss of life, she was awarded the Order of Saint-Charles from Prince Bertrand in a highly formal ceremony in the grand room of the royal palace. She had gone from being a blot on the reputation of the Principality to being its favorite human, all in the space of a few weeks. The French, not to be outdone, decided to award her the Legion of Honor. However, since she had already been awarded this for past heroics, it was agreed she would be promoted to the rank of Grand Officier.

And so it went on for Madelaine for a couple of weeks, but, once all the hullabaloo had settled down, they called her back in to the Monaco Harbor Police Department, shook her hand, and promptly retired her. They didn't officially call it retirement —she was too young—instead it was called a *rest and recuperation period*. Hero she may be, but the genteel ways of the Monaco Police were ill-equipped to handle a loose cannon such as Inspector Madelaine Duchamp. She still retained her rank and, officially at least, she was still part of the force. But, in terms of working, it was more a case of *don't call us, we'll call you.* Not that she cared that much, she was still on full pay, so that suited her just fine. She vowed to enjoy it while it lasted.

By way of a goodbye, Madelaine visited the little dog, Fluffy, in the kennels to see how it was getting on. After all, had it not poked its head out when it did, then the world might well be a different place today. Princess Maud had refused to accept that this bedraggled mutt was her precious canine companion and had effectively abandoned it back into the care of the Monaco Police Department. So the poor creature was shipped off to the station kennels and spent its days in the company of the working dogs. Yet, over time, it was brought back to health by the kind husbandry of Sergeant Jules and the other dog handlers. They had also begun to warm to its canine charms and had considered keeping it as a mascot. Although its name would definitely have to change.

It was ecstatic when it saw Madelaine and ran around her ankles wagging its tail with such an excited vigor it was very likely on the verge of passing out. Its obvious delight in seeing her cracked open the hard shell of Madelaine's emotional protective layer and, in the end, she couldn't leave it there. She just didn't have the heart, so she brought it home, a leaving present of sorts. Leon was delighted.

As for Charles, he had been subjected to a grueling series of interviews and debriefing sessions by the French authorities, who were trying to piece together the sequence events that led to the sabotage attempt on ITER. For his troubles, he was living as a guest of the French state in Nice, pending his return home.

Even though Madelaine had obligations to attend to in Monaco, they were never apart for too long. Then, after a celebratory dinner for them organized by the ITER directorship —where an overindulgent quantity of wine was consumed by both—they became more than just good friends. A few weeks later, Charles was giving her a tour of a new yacht he had procured, berthed in Nice harbor, and outlining the broad strokes of a new trip he was planning—which would be even better if there was someone to share it with. Madelaine didn't hesitate to accept—it was time for a new, less dangerous, adventure.

She turned the page of her book and the little dog lifted up its head, gave a satisfied yawn, and promptly went back to sleep. She patted its head. "There, there. You go back to sleep now."

Her phone chimed. She reached over, picked it up from the salon table, and read the screen. It was Régis, her former boss. She swiped her thumb and answered.

"Don't tell me you're missing me already?" she said.

"Ha, Madelaine, it's so quiet and peaceful around here without you. Nobody has wrecked a helicopter in ages. Anyway, I just wanted to give you a heads up, since you're out of the loop these days, so to speak. Xiang Zu was assassinated this morning in Algiers. Someone nailed him in the market, a single sniper shot."

"Really? Algiers? Are they sure it's him?"

"Oh, it's him alright."

"Any details on who pulled the trigger?"

"None, could be any number of people, he did have a pretty sizable collection of enemies. Just thought you'd like to know."

"Yeah, thanks. It's hard to believe. I thought he had gone to ground."

"Well, he's in the ground now for sure."

Madelaine laughed.

"So, how's retirement?" Régis asked, a little mockingly.

"Great, you should try it some time."

"Someday, Madelaine, someday. But, unfortunately, I'm too young to retire and too lazy to be a hero. Anyway, got to go. Some of us have work to do."

"Okay, and thanks."

"And give my regards to Leon."

"Will do... bye."

Madelaine put the phone down. *So they nailed the bastard.* She smiled.

Zizz... zizz...

She jumped in her seat when she heard the sound. Panicked, she turned to find its source—it was coming from just outside the salon hatchway. She looked around for something to use as a weapon, anything—she could hear it getting closer. The little dog felt her fear and jumped down from the seat. It stood foursquare on the floor looking out the open hatch, its body rigid, all senses on high alert. Just then, a small plastic quad-copter came buzzing through the door, bounced around the yacht interior, and ended upside down on the floor. The little dog barked and danced around it. Then Leon came running in holding a set of controls. "Look what Charlie got me, it's a camera drone."

Madelaine was busy trying to get her heart rate back to normal. She picked up the dog. "That's great, Leon, now can you take it outside please."

"Okay." He picked it up, examined it for damage, and shuffled off outside just as Charles came down the companionway steps. He held up two shopping bags. "Breakfast?"

"Goddammit, Charlie, that scared the crap out of me."

"Oops... sorry." He gave an apologetic smile. "There's a guy selling them down in the market, I couldn't resist. It's just cheap Chinese tech anyway." He smiled again. "I've got some fresh sardines, caught this morning."

Madelaine put the dog down and gave him an affectionate embrace. "Breakfast sounds great."

Charles started unpacking the bags.

"Speaking of cheap Chinese tech," said Madelaine. "I just got a call from Régis"

"Don't tell me, they can't live without you?"

"Xiang Zu was assassinated this morning in Algiers."

Charles looked over at her. "Wow, I didn't see that coming. Any idea who did it?"

"Nothing official. It could be any of a number of people. The Chinese state maybe, they didn't like the way he was operating, he was getting too powerful. Maybe the ITER event was the last straw for them."

"What about the Americans? Now that they found out that the disaster at Livermore wasn't an accident."

"Of course, there's always a possibility it was the French. In the end we may never know who did it." She shrugged her shoulders.

Charles dumped the sardines in the sink.

"I don't suppose it matters now anyway," she continued.

"No, but I for one will sleep a lot better knowing he's gone." He placed the fish on a board and seasoned them.

"You know, Charlie, there's one other thing that still puzzles me."

"Yeah, what's that?"

"Why me, why did you call me and not some other officer at the station?"

"Well, that's easy." He began putting the sardines into a pan on the cooker. They sizzled and spat as he prodded them with a fork.

"I looked up the website for the Monaco Harbor Police and found a group photo of the team. You just looked so hot and sexy that I thought, hey, I might get lucky here if I played my cards right."

"Ha, ha, yeah, right. Seriously though."

"What, you don't believe me?" he laughed.

"No."

He turned the fish, prodded them again and put the fork down. "Okay, if you really want to know. I needed to find someone that might actually run with the tip-off I was giving. Remember, I was making an anonymous call. So I picked out the officers with sufficient rank and then studied the faces from the team photo. Yours just had that look, a kind of gritty, determined look."

"That's the reason?"

"That's it."

"I knew it."

"Knew what?"

"I always knew trouble had a way of finding me."

THE END

ALSO BY GERALD M. KILBY

If you like fast-paced scifi thrillers then why not check out some of my other books.

COLONY MARS: SIX BOOK SERIES

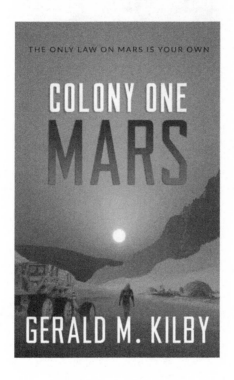

COLONY ONE MARS

How can a colony on Mars survive when the greatest danger on the planet is humanity itself?

THE BELT: SIX BOOK SERIES

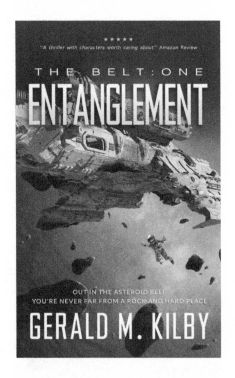

ENTANGLEMENT

Out in the asteroid belt, you're never far from a rock and a hard place.

ABOUT THE AUTHOR

Gerald M. Kilby grew up on a diet of Isaac Asimov, Arthur C. Clark, and Frank Herbert, which developed into a taste for Iain M. Banks and everything ever written by Neal Stephenson. Understandable then, that he should choose science fiction as his weapon of choice when entering the fray of storytelling.

CHAIN REACTION is his first novel and is very much in the old-school techno-thriller style while his latest books, **COLONY MARS** and **THE BELT,** are both best sellers, topping Amazon charts for Hard Science Fiction and Space Exploration.

He lives in the city of Dublin, Ireland, in the same neighborhood as Bram Stoker and can be sometimes seen tapping away on a laptop in the local cafe with his dog Loki.

You can connect with Gerald M. Kilby at:
www.geraldmkilby.com

Made in United States
North Haven, CT
02 May 2022

18784189R00161